This book is a work of fiction. Names of businesses, organizations, places and characters are the product of the authors' imaginations and not to be confused with real people, businessess, places or organizations. Any resemblances are purely coincidental.

ISBN: 1-4679-7247-9
ISBN-13: 978-1-4679-7247-5

PROLOGUE

The bell rang for lunch. RJ looked up at the clock and then at Mr. Kohla. Mr. Kohla finished what he was saying about the Mountains in Utah, but RJ didn't hear anything because his heart was beating so fast. He looked over at Becky. She was two rows over and three back. She had a little smile on her face, but she looked straight ahead.

"All right," Mr. Kohla said, "have a good lunch. See you tomorrow."

Usually there was talking and laughing, but we all went into the hall and quietly found our lockers.

Mr. Kohla followed us into the hall. He had his bag lunch with him. "Are you guys OK?" he asked. "You haven't been this quiet since the first day of school."

"Maybe we're just tired," said Becky.

Several people said, "yes."

"OK, then let's go."

Everyone put their books in the lockers and walked down the hall to the cafeteria. The two other eighth grade classes were also in the hall. They were quiet as well.

When they reached the cafeteria, they all stood against the long wall, waiting for the lunch line to open. The cafeteria was empty. All the tables were clean. They were the first lunch of the day, so even Mr. Hurley, the custodian, had nothing to do. He stood in the far corner with his wash cloth, bucket, and mop. It was just another day at Blalock Middle School. But it wasn't another ordinary day. Near the door farthest from the kitchen was the teachers' table. It was full. There were five eighth-grade teachers, including Mr. Kohla, Mr. Simpson, the gym teacher, Mrs. Gallagher, the counselor, three teacher aides, and Mrs. Reardon, the principal. They were opening their bag lunches and talking as they always did. But today was not ordinary. And the teachers noticed something. It was quiet. It was supposed to be quiet, but not this quiet. One at a time, they stopped lunch preparations and looked around the cafeteria. Each of them wanted to say something, but they didn't know what to say.

The sound of the folding screen that opened the serving line and the kitchen seemed particularly loud. Two of the teachers actually jumped.

The line ladies were in a row: one for the meals, one for the dessert, one for snacks, and one for the drinks. They were startled by the children: not that they didn't see them every day, but never in total silence. Mrs. Gallagher stood up. That usually meant she was going to blow her whistle for silence so she could tell all the children they were being too loud. But she just held the whistle because it had no use.

"There are no kids who brought their lunches," said Mr. Hurley. He thought he was whispering, but today it was the loudest sound in the room.

And he was right. All the tables were empty because everyone in the eighth grade was in line for the school lunch.

Mrs. Reardon was about to say something, if she could think of something to say. But nothing came to mind.

Finally the first lunch lady said, "Well, come and get your food." But no one did.

Instead, every student reached into a pocket or purse or pencil bag and took out a piece of paper. It was small, maybe three or four inches square. Then, the students all began to unwrap their pieces of paper. They did it slowly and deliberately. No one hurried. When the papers were unfolded, they were regular-sized computer paper. The students held the papers straight out in front of them. The papers were blank. The teachers' mouths were open. Some student—none of the teachers could say whom—turned and faced the center of the cafeteria. The teachers looked down the long line of three classes of eighth graders. Then all at once, the students turned over the papers. Each one was identical. One word in bold black letters stood in the middle of each page: NO.

.

SIX HOURS LATER
NBC STUDIOS
NEW YORK

"Good evening from New York. This is the "NBC Nightly News" with Celia Roberts. First up tonight, an absolutely fascinating story about seventh and eighth graders. At lunch today in more than one hundred schools across the nation, seventh and eighth grade students didn't eat the school lunches. A little odd, but not particularly newsworthy you might say, but it was the way they did it. In every school that we have been able to contact, all the seventh and eighth graders came to school with no lunches from home. Then they lined up in the cafeterias and without a word took out pieces of computer paper on which there was one word: NO. When teachers and parents asked the students the meaning of their stance, the teens said that they would no longer eat school lunches. When asked specifically why, all the students we spoke to told us that they knew the cafeteria food wasn't good for them and would likely make them overweight and maybe even sick."

"So, how did they come to this conclusion, and how could they organize such an event? We have some, but not all, of the answers. Here's Carl Sandista from our affiliate in San Francisco."

"Thank you, Celia. Here at Jack London Middle School in Tiburon, California, eighth-grade students went without lunch today.

With the permission of her parents, I talked to Emily Kwo, a student here, about it."

Carl: "Emily, why the boycott on school lunches?"

Emily: "Well, all of us here have been studying nutrition and specifically how poor diets are making kids fat and even obese in this country. We also have found out that a lot of what is in our school lunches is not very good for us."

Carl: "Did you learn that in school?"

Emily: "Some of it we learned in science class, but most of it we have found on the Internet and postings from other kids in the country plus the stuff that's been in the news about lunches in the last few weeks.

Carl: "Emily, how did you get the information from the Internet?

Emily: "There has been a lot of sharing of information about this by kids across the country. I learned about it from students in Florida who have a website called "Good Food for Good Kids," and another one is called "schoollunchbox.org." But there are others."

Carl: "Last question, Emily. How did all you kids know to do what you did today? Someone had to organize it."

Emily: "I guess, but I don't really know. Some of us got e-mails last week from a kid who calls himself BFFKids. He has a site called BFFKids.org. I read it a lot. He explained what people were going to do. He said not to tell adults because they would think it was just kids fooling around, and it's not."

Carl: "So is there anything else you can tell us?"

Emily: "Not really."

"So there you have it, Celia, from the mouths of babes."

"Thanks, Carl. There has been some speculation that this was part of a plan by 8th Day, a loosely knit group, some say a radical group, of college professors, students, and other adults across the country who have been lobbying for better nutrition for school kids. They have taken on the food industry in public through ad campaigns and TV spots along with sit-in's and protests, mostly at fast food restaurants and food industry buildings. Over the last week and a half, e-mails, internal memos, and reports that have cast doubt on the nutritional value of school lunch programs across the country have been leaked to the press. The government entities and private companies who were the target of the leaks have so far denied or not commented on the validity of the accusations. There have been threats of lawsuits and criminal action against 8th Day from the industry, but so far nothing concrete. 8th Day says it welcomes an open investigation and discussion about the leaked documents, but they claim no connection to today's protest. At any rate, this may be the biggest organized protest since the '60's. I think I'll get my tie-dyed shirts and love beads out of storage. And now for the rest of the news…"

BLALOCK MIDDLE SCHOOL
LUNCHTIME

"No? No what?" Mrs. Reardon had walked over to the line of children. For a moment no one said anything. Finally Becky Albright said, "No more school lunches."

RJ was so glad Becky had put herself in charge of things. That way neither he nor the other three could be identified as the leaders. Becky had actually thought she was in charge.

"And why not?" asked Mrs. Reardon.

"Because they make us fat and unhealthy."

"I knew it. This is all about that science fair project that you and RJ sneaked in. Who told you to do this?"

"We saw it on the Internet," said Donny Scott.

"So who organized it?" Mrs. Reardon was losing her temper.

"We don't know," said Becky. "We all just saw it on BFFKids, a site that kids use. It was posted a few days ago."

"And what makes you think the lunches are bad. That silly project you and RJ did?" Her face was starting to turn red. Someone giggled but quickly fell silent.

"Not just that, from school and lots of other places."

"School?" said Mrs. Reardon. RJ looked over and thought Mr. Kohla was going to choke.

"Sure, we learn about what's good to eat. But, no, the teachers didn't tell us about school lunches. We found out about that on the Internet."

"On the Internet?"

"Yes. We've been reading about those documents and e-mails that have been in the newspapers. There's lots of other sites too, but I like schoollunchbox.org."

"And you don't know who organized this little … …protest?"

"No. And it's not a protest. It's just making a statement."

"Well, I've got a statement I want to make. Get rid of these signs and go back to class. No lunch or recess today. And, I will be calling your parents."

8TH Day

EXPOSE, DISCLOSE, REFORM
MISSION STATEMENT

8th Day is a nonprofit, grass roots, Internet-based organization dedicated to exposing health-related injustices, disclosing the truth about these injustices, and bringing about reform. Our mission is to provide transparency in an era when special interest groups dominate. We consist of educators, journalists, and grass roots activists working to expose, disclose, and bring about reform. We provide a secure and anonymous way for independent sources around the world to disclose information to journalists. We keep the identity of our sources confidential and provide a means for revealing suppressed and censored information.

CHAPTER ONE

My parents argue a lot. At least they used to. Then they got divorced.

It was Thursday afternoon and the next day was the last before our spring break. I was sitting at my computer playing *The Galaxy of Death* when I heard the door open. I knew it couldn't be mom because she was working, and I wasn't supposed to have people over when she wasn't home.

"Hey! Where is everybody?" Right away I knew it was my brother. Ryan is lots older than me. He's a freshman at Columbia University in New York. When he was my age, his friends called him RJ, but when he went to high school he wanted to use Ryan. So he started calling me RJ, and now everyone does. I like it because before I was Robbie, and that sounds like a little kid's name. Besides, Ryan is such a cool guy; I want to be just like him.

"In my room," I yelled back. I turned off the computer quickly because he doesn't like *The Galaxy of Death*.

"Well, get out here. It's your biggest, best brother." I got up and went into the living room.

1

"Yeah, my only brother." Ryan is very tall and thin, and I hope to grow as tall as him some day. I'm only about average for my age right now. He played basketball and baseball in high school. He walked over to me, grabbed me, and pulled me up.

"No kiss for your big and handsome brother?" He still likes to kiss me, and it's OK in private but not around my friends. He kissed me on the top of my head and messed up my hair. I tried to pull away, but he held on. It's a game we play. I really like it. He's my best friend.

"So where's mom?"

"She is at Shenanigans. You just missed her. She got home from school and went right back out."

After the divorce, Mom and I moved to Blalock, Tennessee, so she could work at the university here. Aunt Lucy lives in the next town. She's Mom's sister, and she told Mom about the job. Mom is a bookkeeper for the athletics department. My dad is still in Connecticut where we lived before.

Mom is also a waitress at a restaurant in town. We need the money because dad lost his job in New York. He's living with my Grandpa and Grandma, and he can't pay any alimony. Ryan is on a scholarship and has to work so he can stay in school.

"So how's it going big guy? Missed me? I thought a visit here over spring break would be fun. I saw Dad before I left the city, and he says hello. He wishes he could talk to you more."

"I'd like that, too, but Mom still gets angry when Dad calls. Even after a year, she's on him about the money for me. And he gets angry with her for moving so far away. Anyway, I miss him, but sometimes talking with him isn't much fun. He's always asking about mom. I don't know what to say."

"Well, mom should be happy to see me. By the way, big guy, you *are* getting to be a big guy."

"Thanks, Ryan."

"It wasn't entirely a compliment. Yes, you're taller and older, but it looks like you've put on some pounds. Aren't you playing any sports here?"

"Not so much; none of my friends like sports much." He was right. I have been getting heavier, and it stinks. Some of the jerks whose parents work at the university have started to call me Pudge. I almost got in a fight over that with Austin, but the teachers stopped it. Also, I don't want to worry mom. She worries too much already.

"But you always liked sports. I remember you in Little League and Pop Warner. You were really good. Remember how we used to play catch with Dad? You never wanted to stop."

"I know, but most of the kids who play sports here are the ones whose parents are professors at the university. The rest of us don't."

"Who's us, and why don't you play?"

"I don't really know, but the professors kids hang out together, and they don't talk to anybody else. They think they're better than we are. They call us townies. So they stay to themselves and we stay to ourselves."

"But Mom works at the university."

"She's just a bookkeeper, and she says most of the professors never talk to her either."

"Yeah, I get it. I see some of that at my school. But I have another question for you, RJ. What have you been eating?"

"What's this all about?"

"Just humor me. I have a secret to tell you when you answer some questions."

"Why is it a secret? You always tell me everything."

"Not always."

"Like what?"

"Like what was going on with Mom and Dad."

"You knew what was going on?"

"Pretty much. They tried to hide it from you, but they talked to me because I was old enough. Boy, that sucked."

"What do you mean?"

"It's not important now. I love them both, but it was hard when they were breaking up."

"You should have told me."

"Yeah, maybe, but it didn't seem like a good idea at the time. Let's get back to my question. You do want to hear the secret don't you?"

"I suppose. What do you want to know?"

"Just what you've been eating since you moved down here. Stuff that's different from when we were all together."

"That's hard. Well, mom brings a lot of stuff from restaurants because she gets home late and she's so tired."

"So not as many sit-down dinners made by mom?"

"Not really. Actually, sometimes we don't eat together because she's so tired. She just leaves the food on the table and lies down."

"So what's the food like?"

"You know, burgers, fries, sometimes chicken, and sometimes pizza."

"What are you drinking?

"Cokes, mainly, and Sunkist."

"What about milk and juices?"

"Mom has some juice in the fridge, but I like soda better. I drink milk with my cereal at breakfast, if I eat breakfast."

"If?"

"Sometimes we're in too much of a hurry."

"What about… No, that's enough. I get the picture. And it's all about the secret I have to tell you. Listen to me, big guy. This is a real no-phony-baloney secret. Can you handle it? It means not telling mom."

"But what could it be that mom shouldn't know? I'm not sure I like keeping secrets from mom."

"I know you don't, and I don't either. That's one of the things that makes you such a great brother and son, but you'll have to trust me on this one. I promise you this will not hurt mom; it will probably help her. Do you believe me?"

"Of course, but…"

"You have my word. Give me your pinky."

"I'm too old for that."

"You're never going to be older than me, so let's see it."

We hadn't done a pinky swear since I was in first grade. He told me it was a thing that all his friends did when they were just little kids. He still liked to do it with me, and it was something special we shared. I thought I had grown out of it, but I linked my pinky with his.

"I, Ryan Johnson, swear that what I will tell you will not hurt mom. Now you swear that you won't tell anyone. And by the way, if after you hear the secret, you don't want to be part of it, that's OK. Just don't tell anyone."

I thought about it. I didn't like not telling mom, but this was Ryan. He has always taken care of me, and he's the best brother I could hope for.

"I swear," I said, and we pulled our pinkies apart. "This better be a big deal."

"The biggest," he answered..

CHAPTER TWO

THURSDAY, APRIL 7TH
RJ

When I was very young, Ryan was like a second father. He took me places, played ball with me, and told me what I should and shouldn't do; I loved it. But now that he was asking me not to tell something to mom, it bothered me a little. What could be such a big deal that she couldn't know? But there was only one way to find out. So I promised to keep it a secret.

"Have you heard of 8th Day?"

"I think I might have heard that name on TV, but I don't remember why."

"It's a group of people from all over the country who are worried about the health of young people. The group does really important things to help save people."

"Save them from what?"

"Food companies, bad restaurants, drug companies, and mainly themselves."

"I don't understand. What does 8th Day mean, and what does 8th Day do? And what is wrong with these companies? And why don't I know about it. And are you part of it?"

"Slow down, big guy. One thing at a time."

"First, 8th Day gets its name from the Bible. Remember, the world was supposed to be created in seven days. So this is the 8th Day—the day we make the world better. The way it should be. Yes, I'm part of it. It's a huge group with thousands of members: college kids, professors, nutritionists, and other adults who just want to help. The group does a lot of things. They have monthly newsletters and a website; they write letters to newspapers; they hand out information about health; they write people in Congress about the health problems our country has to deal with, and many other things. Sometimes they picket fast food places like Clown Burger or even the headquarters of food companies."

"Picketing? Like what they did in the 60's? I learned about that in school. They were called hippies, right? They had long hair and wore weird clothes. They had sit-ins at colleges, and restaurants and other places. But I never really got the whole story. I know they were against the Vietnam War and everything."

"Hold on, RJ. You're right, mostly. They were all about change. The war in Vietnam was shortened because of them. But they also helped black people get to use their right to vote, and they were part of the women's movement for equality."

"So, now you're doing that. Why?"

"First of all, it's a family tradition. Remember those pictures of Grandpa and Grandma Johnson?"

"Oh yeah, I remember, they had the long hair and funny shirts and wore love beads."

"Yes, they were part of the movement and they got arrested at a sit-in."

"No way."

"Oh, yes. They helped make a difference in this country. Now I want to make a difference, and I'm asking you for help."

"Am I going to picket and maybe go to jail? I don't think Mom would like that."

"Absolutely not, but you would be doing something very important that would help the cause. There are new things that need to be done now. This time it's all about health; people young and old need to help. We need to make some changes and make them now or many more kids are going to get diseases that only older people used to get. It's already starting, and it's very scary to see kids your age get those diseases."

"What do you mean?"

"Well you know that Poppie has diabetes, right?"

"Yeah and he has to check his blood sugar three times a day, and I can't watch it. I've seen him get sick and have to sit down after dinner. He says he shouldn't eat cake, but he does and it makes him sick."

"I hate that, too, RJ. Remember the time Nan had a heart attack and had to go to the hospital? What's really frightening is that people your age are getting diseases that used to only be part of getting old."

"I know a guy in my grade who had to go to the hospital because he couldn't breathe. He's very fat, and I heard that the doctors wanted him to lose weight, but he hasn't yet," I said. "What can I do, and what are you doing?"

"Well, like I said before, we have been picketing fast food restaurants and food companies, posting things on our website, and writing things we hope the TV stations and newspapers will show to people. So far we haven't had much luck getting people to pay attention. That's where you come in."

"I do?"

"Yes. Right now the people who run the food services in this country are ignoring us because we're just college kids, professors, and nutritionists, and the companies think that older people won't pay much attention. And so far they have been right. But with your help and help from some other people, we may be able to change that."

"How? If they won't listen to you, why would they listen to me?"

"Pretty simple. Older people—moms, dads, and grandparents—worry more about kids your age than they do about college-age kids. They don't take us seriously, and they think when we leave college and get jobs we might forget all this bad stuff. And maybe they're right. That's why 8th Day has decided to try two new things. The first part has nothing to do with you; some of the college members are going to do some things that will really annoy the food companies. They are going to be a part of 8th Day, but no one will know who they are. It will be a secret because if they get caught, the college kids might even get arrested."

"Wow. They're taking a big chance."

"Yes, they are. The second part is about you. What we are going to ask you and some others to do is absolutely safe. But you guys in school can go places I can't and find out things we can't."

"What do you mean?"

Ryan looked at his watch. "We'll talk more about that later. Are you willing to help?"

"I suppose so, maybe. Yes, I will. If Grandma and Grandpa could do this, so can I."

"Good! Well first let me tell you that you are going to be a part of a team. Some other members of 8th Day are talking to their brothers and sisters right now, setting up the team. Your other team members will be from far away. They will live in other states. When they are chosen, you will communicate with each other using your computer and video conferencing."

"Like Skype?"

"Exactly," Ryan said, "but it will be one part of several ways to communicate with your group, so no one can listen in or find out who you are."

"You mean like spies?"

"Kinda, except you won't be spying so much as researching, collecting information for us to use in 8th Day's campaign."

"Like what?"

"That's all for today. Mom will be home soon, and I don't want her to hear what we're talking about. Remember, it's a secret, even from Mom."

"Will I ever be able to tell her?" I asked.

"We'll see. I'm staying at Aunt Lucy's cause they have more room. I'll see you soon. Tell Mom I love her and I'll see her Saturday."

And then Ryan gave me a kiss on the top of my head and went out the front door. I got up and watched him get on his motorcycle and drive away.

CHAPTER THREE

THURSDAY, APRIL 7TH

RJ

Our house is small, a lot smaller than the one we had in Connecticut. But it's OK for just mom and me. But I miss the big yard we had. Now there is just a little bit of space in the front, and the grass doesn't grow very well because of the big trees. The back yard is tiny and has one of those wood fences mom calls a stockade fence. Some kids from the college use the house in the back. It's so close that we can hear them when they have parties, which is pretty much every weekend.

In Connecticut we had four acres. Most of it was wooded, but there was a large lawn around the house, plenty of room to play ball or hide-and-seek or just walk in the woods. Dad took real good care of the lawn. He hung a tire swing from a big old tree in the back yard. Ryan used it first; then it was mine. Dad and Ryan would swing me in the evenings. I loved it. I didn't want them to stop, not even when it got dark. But then we would go in and mom would have dinner ready. We all sat together and talked. I loved listening to Ryan tell us about high school.

Then everything changed just after Ryan graduated and was about to go to college. Dad was home a lot, and when I asked why, he told me he was changing jobs and would have a new job soon; until then it would be like a vacation.

All of a sudden, Mom and Dad seemed angry all the time. I heard them yelling at each other and I would run down from my room to see what was happening. But they stopped when I came in the room. They always answered "nothing" when I asked what was happening. It seemed to get worse very fast. I stopped checking on them, closed the door to my room, and put a pillow over my head to mute them out, but I could still hear. My pillow would be wet from my crying.

One time Ryan came in and saw me hiding, and he sat on the bed and talked to me. Ryan told me Dad had lost his job and there wasn't much money, which made Dad mad and made Mom worry. He told me Mom and Dad were having problems, but it wasn't my fault or his. I wondered how he knew that I thought I had done something wrong.

"Do you cry too?" I asked.

"Sometimes," he answered, "but it doesn't help."

When he said that, Ryan looked really sad and angry. I had never seen him that way before.

"Whose fault is it?" I asked.

"I don't know. I get angry with Dad because he should be taking care of Mom and us. But I don't really know what he can do or why they can't be nice to each other."

Then everything happened so fast. Ryan went to college, Mom cried, and Dad looked really sad. Mom told me they were selling the house and she and I were moving to Tennessee because she had found a job there. When I asked her about Dad, she looked away and said Dad was going to stay with Grandma and Grandpa.

"When will he come to be with us?"

"I don't know," Mom said as she turned her head. I could tell she was crying. And my chest felt tight.

So now we live in Tennessee and it's OK. After we had lived here for almost a year, Mom and Dad got a divorce and I felt so empty; I couldn't talk for days. Mom wanted me to see a counselor at school, but I just yelled "no" at her. I had never yelled at her before. But she didn't make me see anyone. I guess I got used to our new life, but I can't say I like it a lot.

Mom got home at ten o'clock. She looked tired.

"What did you eat for dinner?" she asked.

"Some of that chicken from The Happy Clucker."

"Did you have any vegetables?"

"Just the french fries."

She just sighed and put her hand on my face.

"I'll get some things for a salad and put them in the refrigerator. Promise me you'll eat it."

"Yes, Mom. Oh, Ryan's here. He's staying at Aunt Lucy's because they have more room. He said he'd come over Saturday morning to see you."

"Oh, this is his break. I forgot. How does he look?"

"He looks great."

"What did you guys talk about?"

I felt uncomfortable.

"Oh, just stuff. I really miss him."

"Me too."

"Actually we did talk about something I wanted to ask you about."

"What's that?"

"He was telling me how Grandma and Grandpa Johnson used to protest and picket and things, but I really didn't understand."

"Why was he talking about that?"

"Oh, I just asked about a picture I saw of them and they were dressed funny and were carrying signs." It didn't feel good not telling her the whole truth.

"Well, it was a very different time. Your grandparents were hippies." She smiled when she said it.

"That's what I thought. We learned about them in school."

"Well they were, and they believed they could improve social injustices by making a stand. Some people thought they were being silly; others took them very seriously. But there is no doubt they changed things, and some of it was very good."

"Ryan said they got arrested once. I just can't see Grandma and Grandpa doing anything so bad that they would get arrested."

She laughed. "Yeah, I understand, but they were doing something they believed was very important, and if they had to do things that might get them in trouble that was OK with them. And you need to know they never ever did anything to hurt anyone. I think you should be proud of them."

"Were Nan and Poppie hippies too?"

"No, my parents were poor, and they had to go to work after high school. Poppie had to go into the army for a few years. Later on they both went to college at night, so they could make more money for our family." She sighed as if she were thinking about something important.

"I'm tired, honey. It's time we both went to bed."

And we did.

CHAPTER FOUR

FRIDAY, APRIL 8TH

RJ

The next day was Friday. It was the last day before spring break. Mr. Kohla's eighth grade class had a party. We call Mr. K. The Bear because of his name. He is pretty heavy though and looks a lot like a bear with his beard and long hair. At the party, we had food that our moms' sent in. There was lots of pizza and soda and donuts and candy. I was having a good time, but I started thinking about what Ryan said about my weight. I wasn't so hungry even though I love pizza.

I noticed the kids from the university didn't eat much; they hardly touched the candy. And the stuff their moms' sent in was different. Some of my friends called it weird. They had tomato sandwiches and raw carrots and some strange drinks I hadn't heard of. I decided to try some of their stuff because we could eat anything we wanted, and it tasted OK. But my friends called me stupid for eating the snob food, and the university kids looked at me like I didn't belong. But that's nothing new.

The party was fun, but I was excited to have a whole week off. I was looking forward to seeing Ryan. He was going to take care of me on Saturday while mom worked at Shenanigan's. I was hoping for a ride on his motorcycle.

I heard him before I saw him. He parked the bike in the front yard, took off his helmet, and came in. Mom was waiting for him.

"Ryan," she said and then hugged him real hard and put her head on his chest. He's almost a foot taller than she is.

"I can't believe my baby is so big." She pushed away and looked at him. "You look skinny. Aren't you eating?"

"I'm in perfect health," he said. "But you look a little tired."

He was right; Mom always looks tired.

"Oh, I just haven't woken up yet."

"Hey, big guy," he said to me, "go get ready, and I'll talk to Mom for a bit."

I went to my room and grabbed the helmet Ryan got me for Christmas. I put on a sweatshirt because it can be cold on the bike. I noticed the sweatshirt felt a little small.

When I got back to the living room, Mom was putting on the apron she wore to work and was getting ready to leave.

"Now you take care of your little brother," she told Ryan. "And you do what your brother says," she told me. "I don't want you two getting into trouble."

"You can count on me," he said.

"I'll do whatever he tells me, Mom. You know I always do."

"I know." Then she looked at us together, and I thought she was getting sad again. But she grabbed her purse and went out the door.

"You ready for some adventure?" he asked.

"I was born ready." I always say that because it's something Ryan used to say.

We took the motorcycle right down University Avenue. I saw some kids from my class, but they didn't wave. They just stared with their mouths open. *Good*, I thought. We took the long ride out to Palmer Lake where they have the fireworks on the Fourth of July. He parked the bike, and we walked to the dock and hung our legs over the edge. No one else was around. There were some ducks on the lake, and they swam toward us hoping for some food.

"OK, let's talk about what I need you to do."

"Before you start," I said, "what did you mean about me getting fat?"

"I didn't say you were fat. But you have gained weight, and I am concerned that you're not eating right. And that's part of why I need your help. Remember when we talked about how kids are getting illnesses that used to be only for old people? Well we know that it has a lot to do with being overweight. Almost half of the kids your age in this country are overweight, and 20 percent are obese."

"I heard about being obese on TV, but isn't that like being humungous-like you can't even walk?"

"For boys it's like when one quarter of their weight is fat. So if you were one hundred pounds, twenty-five of those pounds would be fat. For girls it's a little different. They would have to have one third of their weight as fat to be obese."

"So what does that mean?"

"How many kids in your class?"

"Twenty-five. That's in homeroom."

"OK, that means," said Ryan, "probably about five kids in the class. Think about your class. Does that number make sense? Remember, I'm talking about really overweight."

I thought for a minute. "I think I can count seven, but I'm not exactly sure."

"Close enough," said Ryan. "And by the way, of those seven how many university kids?"

"None," I said. "But what does that mean?"

"Could mean a lot of things, but it usually has everything to do with what and how much people eat. And how much exercise they get."

"So are you saying the university kids are smarter or better?" I didn't like this.

"Absolutely not. Lucky is more like it."

"Lucky about what?"

"I'm guessing that somewhere along the line they were taught to eat healthy food, but they don't spend too much time thinking about it."

"I still don't like them. They're not nice to me."

"Not nice is a bad thing, too."

"Being obese or just overweight can cause lots of bad things. It can make you sick like Poppie and Nan; it can cause breathing problems; it can hurt your work in school; and it will definitely cause you to die earlier than you should."

"You're scaring me, Ryan."

"Sorry, big guy, I don't want to scare you, but I do want you to know the truth so you can help yourself."

"But doesn't Mom take good care of me?"

"Of course she does, but she is so busy that she has to spend all of her time making enough money for you guys to live. Plus, not all adults know a lot about obesity either. Over twenty-five percent of them are obese, too."

"I just thought people got fatter when they got older. Most of my friend's parents are a little fat and their grandparents are fatter than that."

"I know, but what about Grandma and Grandpa? Are they fat?"

"No," I admitted. "But Nan and Poppie are a little."

"True," he said. "One of the most important things 8th Day does is teach people the importance of eating right and eating only good food. But people aren't listening to us, RJ. I need to do something to try to change it just like Grandpa and Grandma did in the '60s. We need help. You can get us important information that can change the lives of millions of kids."

"I could do that?"

"Absolutely."

"OK, tell me what I need to do."

CHAPTER FIVE

SATURDAY, APRIL 9
LAMAR

My sister, Jeane, is a senior at George Washington High School. I want to go there when I reach ninth grade. But my Mama warned me that it might not happen.

She said, "You never know what's goin' on here in Detroit these days. They move kids from school to school all the time, particularly schools with mostly black kids. The city is in such bad shape, and the people in charge didn't think much about us when times were good. Now they ain't so good. So don't you go countin' on anything. Just do your best and find a way to get out of this place." Mama is shorter than me, and she has gained some weight recently. I can tell she has a hard time walking sometimes, but she never complains. She may be short, but when she talks everyone listens. She's not loud; she just gets your attention.

But I still hope I can go there. Jeane is an honor student. It looks like she'll get a scholarship to Wayne State. Actually, she has been taking summer classes there for the last two years. That's where she met Rashon. He's a sophomore at Wayne State. I can tell he likes her a lot. And he should. She is smart and very pretty with dark eyes, light skin, and midnight hair done in dreadlocks.

We are brother and sister, but we don't look like each other. Mama says I got my Dad's genes. I'm tall and skinny with darker skin. I keep my hair really short. I'd shave my head, but Mama says no.

I like Rashon. He's always nice to me, and it's good to have a guy around. My dad is dead. He was killed in a car accident when I was only five. I remember him sometimes, but it was so long ago. I remember Mama being really upset. I was scared for her. But Jeane helped me a lot, and we got on with it.

Dad was a plumber. He owned his own business. When he died Mama said there was a small insurance policy that helped us buy our apartment. Mama used to work for General Motors. She got laid off and now she works at Cullen's department store. She says it's not a great job, but at least she has one. Lots of kids at school have parents who can't find work. But Cullen's stays open late, and Mama mostly works the late shift. Most days she's gone when I get home from school. Jeane takes good care of me. She's a good cook, and she is real strict about us eating healthy meals. She always says, "We don't have a lot, but what we have is good."

"Lamar, are you doing your homework?"

I was sitting at my computer playing a game.

"Already done," I told her.

I don't like to brag, but I am a good student. I have had all A's since I was in kindergarten. It's just easy for me, particularly computers. My computer teacher told me that I know more about them than he does. He's right. I have read everything I can find on computers and love to play around and find sites that other kids have never heard of.

"Good, cause Rashon is coming over later and he wants to talk with you."

"Great." Rashon is always talking to me about what I want to be and what I need to do to get there. He's a biology major and is thinking about applying for medical school.

I like my room. It's small but has everything I need: a bed with Detroit Lions covers, a closet for all my clothes and computer games, posters of Einstein and Wynton Marsalis, and my desk. It's an old wood thing Dad got for me, and he refinished it by hand. Mom told me he got it from a school that closed and was throwing their furniture away. It's really big with three drawers and a hole in the front top that Mom says used to be used for ink. That's a little weird. In the center is my computer. It's an iMac with a 21.5 inch screen, 3.2 Ghz, 1920 by 1080 resolution, 4GB 8 double layer super drive, magic mouse, and a wireless keyboard. It's the best thing I own. And the great thing is I won it. There was a contest at school. I had to write an essay about what motivated me. I wrote about my mom, my sister, and Rashon and about how I needed to do well for my father so I could help the family when I grew up. The PTA read the entries, and I won. I couldn't believe how lucky I was.

Around six o'clock Rashon arrived. I heard him in the kitchen with Jeane. They were kissing and talking silly, so I stayed put. A couple of minutes later, someone tapped on my door.

"Lamar?"

It was Rashon.

"Yeah, man, come on in."

He opened the door and walked in. There wasn't much space because the room is small and he is big. I mean really big. Not fat big, just tall. Maybe six foot six and mostly muscle. He shaved his head and looks like some NBA player, only no tattoos, and his eyes are kind. He sat on my bed and it looked a lot smaller than before.

"How's it goin', buddy?"

I don't really like that name, but I like Rashon too much to say anything. We bumped fists. It was easy to see why sis liked him so much. He was real smart and looked OK, and like I said, he was huge. He could have played basketball, and in fact, he did when he was younger. Some say he could have played in college, but when I asked him he said that the talk was overrated and he wanted to spend more time on his studies. He is like way smart. Sis says it's much more important to be a doctor. I mean Rashon has read more books than I have ever seen. He practically lives in the library. He's taken me to the university library. It is very, very cool—books, magazines, and newspapers all over the place. And then there are the computers. Up until I got mine, they were the best computers I'd ever seen. Rashon helped me with them, but pretty soon I knew more than he did. I read all the computer magazines. Soon I was able to find pretty much anything I wanted on the computer. I actually got myself into the university's system, which is not allowed. I just looked around and got right out, but it felt beastly to be able to do it.

But more than just being smart, Rashon is a great guy. He's like an older brother. He takes me to a lot of places and talks to me a lot. He is always telling me how important school is and that I need to make something of myself because I'm so smart. I hope he's right. He also talks to me about doing the right things.

He said, "Lamar, in everyone's life some things come along that are important, and you have to know what to do then. You have a good heart and you've been raised well by your mom and sister, so all you need to do is look in that heart and you'll know what to do."

I don't know if he's right about everything, but I can remember times that it has worked. One time, a friend, or so I thought, wanted to copy my homework because he knew I got good grades.

I was tempted because sometimes friends are not that easy for me to find, but I knew it was wrong and I learned he was no friend at all.

Don't get me wrong; he can't replace mama and Jeane, who is the best sister a guy could have. She cooks for me, gets me from school, takes me shopping and to the movies. I mean...she's just the best.

"I'm doin' fine, Rashon. How about you?"

"Good, good. School OK?"

"As always," I said.

"Don't doubt it. You are going to be something special, Lamar. You know that don't you?"

"Well..." I stammered.

"Well, I know," he said. "And that's why I want to talk to you about something special. Something you can do to help me and lots of other people."

"Anything for you, Rashon." I couldn't imagine what he could need me for.

"Thanks. This is a big thing, a really big thing, and if you don't want to do it I will understand. Nothing will change between us. You got that?"

"Yes, of course." I was starting to wonder what he had to say.

"First, let me get Jeane in here. She knows about this, and I want to talk to you with her."

Now I was really confused.

"Honey, can you come in here?"

"On my way," she said.

CHAPTER SIX

SATURDAY, APRIL 9
LAMAR

We waited quietly for sis. It was not like Rashon. He liked to talk. He looked a little serious too, but that I got. It's usually when he's going to tell me something he thinks is really important for me to know. And he is usually right.

But what was the deal with sis? If she knows about something, I should know too. We don't have secrets.

"OK," she said as she came in the room. "Sorry, I had to clean some things up for Mom."

She sat on the bed next to Rashon. The room was still quiet. They looked at me. Then they looked at each other.

"You go first, Rashon," she said. He looked at her and then at me.

"You two gotta stop this," I said. "I'm really worried. Is it something about Mama? Please say it's not."

"It's not about Mom, Lamar," said Jeane. "Everything is OK with Mom."

That was a relief.

"But what's all this secret stuff? I'm getting nervous."

My worry made them smile. But just little smiles, not like I'm used to.

Rashon started. "Sorry, buddy. It's an issue we're passionate about, and we have wanted to share with you for a while now. It's very important to us, and we think you will agree. It's so important that we need to know if you can keep it secret."

"Hey," I said, "it's in the family. I can keep a secret in the family."

Jeane made a small frown.

"Well, that's part of it," she said. "This is a thing you can't talk to Mom about."

I was shocked. What in the world could Jeane want to tell me that I couldn't talk about to Mama? After Dad died, we all helped each other. We had no secrets. We had weekly meetings when we shared the day-to-day of our lives. The three of us would sit on Mama's bed on Sunday night and recap the week, sharing the good and the bad. She always said, "there's no need to keep secrets; we're all the same and need each other's help in this world."

Now I'm not supposed to talk to Mama?

"I don't think I like this," I said.

"I can understand," Jeane said, "but there is a good reason. Can I ask a favor?"

"OK," I answered slowly.

"Can you listen to what we have to say, and then you can decide if you want to help us or not? But if you decide not to, I need you to promise not to tell Mom about this talk. Can you do that?"

My mind was running wild, wondering what I had to hide from Mama. I wanted them to go back into the kitchen and pretend this never happened. But that wasn't going to work.

"All right," I said reluctantly.

"Good," said Rashon. They both looked relieved.

"You know about the group 8th Day?" Rashon asked.

"I've read about it on the Internet," I replied. "But I don't know a whole lot. It's a group of people trying to make us healthier."

"Right!" he said. "I'm part of the group."

My eyes got big. "I thought it was a secret group. Aren't they doing things against the law?"

"Not exactly. Some of us are right out in the open. Others are not. I want to tell you about what we are trying to do. We need someone like you to help us."

"Me?" I didn't know what to say. How could a kid my age help? I had read the group was mainly college kids with some older people as well.

"Yes, you. What we need is a person who can handle computers. We need a computer guy who can collect the information we need, but a person nobody would suspect. Someone adults wouldn't take seriously. That would be you. No offense."

"OK."

"Do you remember your Granpapa, Mama's dad?" asked Jeane.

"Yes, of course."

"Remember those stories Mama and Dad used to tell about him?"

"Sure, he was part of the Congress for Racial Equality-CORE. He worked so we could vote and helped people down South. He walked with Dr. King in Selma, Alabama. I tell my class that story every year on Dr. King's birthday," I said.

"Well, are you interested?" asked Rashon. "Can you help like your grandfather did?"

I thought for moment. It sounded a little dangerous, but I sure do love computers, and if Jeane and Rashon were OK with this group's mission, it must be all right. They would never do anything wrong. Besides that's what my Granpapa would have done.

"I'm interested."

"Can you listen now without telling your Mom?"

"Yes, I can do that." I hoped that was the truth.

"Then here it is."

When they were done explaining the details, I was overwhelmed.

"So, are you in?" Jeane asked.

I looked at both of them. "Absolutely."

CHAPTER SEVEN

SATURDAY, APRIL 9
KARSTAN

The doorbell rang. I knew it couldn't be my friends because they would have just walked in. It was Saturday, so it couldn't be Carmella to clean the house; she comes on Monday, Wednesday, and Friday. Besides, she has a key, although she is supposed to knock first. I mean it's not like she would find anyone home but me. Mom and Dad are like never home. And now I'm at level forty-one in *The Galaxy of Death*.

The bell rang again.

I went to the door. It was my Uncle Jerry, so I let him in.

"Hey, K-man, how you doin'?" He always calls me that or Stan the Man. I don't like the nicknames a lot, particularly when he uses them around my friends. My real name is Karstan Peterson.

He always said, "What kind of a name is Karstan? It sounds like a partner in a big law firm; oh, that's right, it is." My mom's family name is Karstan, and she works in granddad's firm, Lloyd, Karstan, and Benson. Uncle Jerry is Dad's brother.

But I love him. He's a great guy, and he has always been around. Actually, I see him almost more than I see Dad or Mom. When I was playing soccer or Little League, he came to all my games, and he was the assistant coach for my baseball team. My dad is a doctor and he works a lot, so he misses a lot of things.

"Whatcha up to?" He gave me a big hug and threw his baseball cap on the railing at the bottom of the stairs. He reached up and pulled the rubber band around his ponytail tighter.

"I was just playing *The Galaxy of Death*."

"I can't understand why you spend so much time on that crap. It rots your brain and makes you lazy. You're a good-looking boy and take after your mom with those blue eyes. But you also have your dad's size. If you ever stood up straight, you'd almost be six feet tall. But who could tell with the baggy pants and too-big t-shirts you wear? It looks like you're hiding inside of your clothes."

"Uncle Jerry, I play less than most of my friends."

"That's not saying much, and what happened to your sports? You were a great second baseman."

"I was just a kid then. None of my friends do that stuff now."

"So get new friends."

"Uncle Jerry…"

"OK, OK," he said, walking into the living room. I paused the game to save my place. We have a big leather chair next to the sofa; it's my father's favorite spot. Uncle Jerry always sits in it when he comes over. He propped his feet on the table in front of the couch. It's an antique and Mom always tells him to take his feet off of it, but he never does.

"It's a beautiful spring day in Connecticut, and you should be outside running around. You have five acres of beautiful lawn and trees, and you're sitting in this two-hundred-year-old, ten-room monstrosity."

"Right," I replied.

"It's an awful thing this world is coming to."

He says that a lot. My mom says he's from outer space. She told me he was born too late to be a hippy, and that is his personal tragedy. He needs to save the whales or the spotted owl or something, or he isn't happy. I don't know about that, but he is different than most older people I know. He has a small store in Westport, down on the Post Road. He sells jewelry that he makes. Dad says he does pretty well because of all the rich people in Westport who have more money than taste. Uncle Jerry has a little house in Fairfield and has lived alone since he divorced. That happened before I was born, so I never met his wife.

"You want something to eat?" he asked as he headed into the kitchen.

"Nah, I'm fine." I went back to playing my game.

A few minutes later, he came back empty-handed.

"Can't believe with all the money your folks have, you can't find a healthy thing to eat in the refrigerator. Not even yogurt. In fact, there's not much of anything at all. What do you people eat?"

"Mom brings a little food home from restaurants, and we eat out a lot."

"I'll bet."

"Mom and Dad are busy. They do important things and work a lot and make a lot of money."

"And your point is?" he asked.

"That's what everyone wants."

"Not everyone," he said.

"Well, you're just weird." Actually, Mom says he's lazy. Dad says he's a free spirit, whatever that means.

"Maybe so," he said. "Tell me, Stan, what are you going to do when you grow up?"

"Uncle Jerry, I'm only in seventh grade."

"Come on. You have thought about it. Everything in this house is planned."

"Well," I said, "I guess I'll go to Brown, choose something to do, and make a lot of money working in New York."

"Just another happy ending," he replied.

"I guess."

"Haven't you ever wanted to do something really important?"

"I really haven't thought about it." I was busy trying to play the game and talk at the same time.

"Well, it's time you did." He turned off the game and looked at me in a way I'd never seen before.

CHAPTER EIGHT

SATURDAY, APRIL 9
KARSTAN

"What's that supposed to mean?"

Uncle Jerry looked serious, which was unusual.

"Money is not everything. Yes, your mom and dad make a lot of money, but they do important stuff too. I know most of your mom's clients are big companies looking to make more and more, but occasionally she takes a case that can really help people. And although the biggest part of your dad's plastic surgery work consists of making rich people look prettier, sometimes he helps burn victims and children with birth defects. You should think about what you can do for others who have less than you, and maybe help yourself along the way."

"What help do I need? And what could I do? I'm only twelve."

"First, you need some help with your health. Look at yourself. Your skin is pale because you hardly ever step foot outside, and although you're not overweight yet, you don't get enough exercise or eat enough decent food. Your future does not look good."

I was confused. Lots of times I didn't really get what Uncle Jerry was saying, but this time I was clueless.

"There are bad things happening to kids your age in this country. Much of it has to do with poor eating habits and lack of exercise."

"Mom always said you were a health nut."

"If that means I care a lot about my health, then I guess I am. But look at me. Your dad and I are about the same age. Who looks younger and fitter?"

No comparison there. Dad had gained a lot of weight. He said he never had time to exercise. Mom wasn't too heavy, but she did look older than Uncle Jerry. Truth is Uncle Jerry looked great for an older guy. He was thin but strong, and he always had a lot of energy. He did dress funny and wear a ponytail though.

"Well, you do, I guess."

"But that's not really the point. I am talking about kids your age. Obesity has grown into an epidemic. Across the country young people are getting fatter and fatter, and as a result, many of them are suffering from bad diseases like diabetes, which used to be considered an old person's illness."

"But what can we do?"

"In my case, I am working for a group called 8th Day. We are trying to get both the general public and the government to do something about the problem."

"Why aren't they doing something already?"

"It's complicated, but mostly it has to do with companies in the food business who are more interested in making money than doing the right thing. In some cases they don't even know the harm they are doing. So I am helping out by writing letters to government officials, and occasionally I take part in an operation like picketing a restaurant to make a point about something."

"Hey, I saw that on TV. Didn't some of them go to jail?"

"No, they were arrested and had to pay a fine, but they didn't go to jail."

"Can I do that stuff? That looks beastly!"

"That's not what we need you for."

"Well, what can I do?"

"It has to do with your mother's law firm."

"Hey, I can't get Mom in trouble."

"No, it's not about her. Her firm represents some food people who are not very nice."

"So what has that got to do with me?"

"Let me tell you."

CHAPTER NINE

SATURDAY, APRIL 9
GRACIELA

April is a busy time in the valley, so many vegetables and fruits to pick. The hours are long, but at least the sun is not as hot as in the summer. I have been picking lettuce every day for a week now. I don't want to see another piece of lettuce for as long as I live! I hope I can pick oranges when I get older because it does not hurt my back as much.

An old pickup truck drove slowly up the long rows.

"*Qué pasa,* my little Graciela?" my uncle asked. He drives the truck where I load up my boxes of lettuce.

"I am good, thank you, Uncle Alberto," I answered.

I always speak English unless I have to speak Spanish. I *am* an American citizen. I was born here thirteen years ago. In fact, I have never been to Mexico, the home of my parents.

"You have done well," Uncle Alberto said. "You have picked much, but it is getting late, and you must go home and do your homework."

"OK," I said.

I removed the big white apron and dusted off my school clothes: blue jeans and a flowered shirt. I am always glad to go home and study. I love school and want to go to college and be a nurse. It will not be easy. My mother, father, and two brothers died in a car accident when I was just seven. My Uncle Alberto and Aunt Belinda took me in. They came to the United States twenty years ago with my parents. They all worked the fields of the beautiful valleys of Southern California. Now my uncle is an assistant manager and oversees many acres of vegetables and fruits. I know they love me, but they have five children of their own, and I don't feel like I fit in exactly. Even though we all work hard, we are not wealthy. We live in a small house just outside the farm. It's a wooden bungalow painted a bright blue. We rent the house from the people who own the farm. It has three bedrooms: one for my aunt and uncle, one for my three boy cousins (Alberto Junior, Candido, and Cesar), and one for the girls (me, Cielo, and Camiria).

The house is crowded, but it's always neat and clean. We all work to keep our home orderly. Little Al, Candy, and Cesar are the oldest, and they're all in high school. Cammy and I attend the middle school. I am in eighth grade, and Cammy is in sixth. Cielo is the baby; she is in second grade. She doesn't work in the fields, but she does help Aunt Belinda around the house after school.

When I arrived, everyone was cleaning up. Then the girls helped with dinner, and the boys cut the lawn and cleaned all the rooms in the house. It was a typical day. Dinner was wonderful. We ate enchiladas (tortillas filled with cheese and sour cream) and beans (frijoles). There was plenty for everyone. My Uncle said a prayer in Spanish. He asked to bless the house and his family and this great country where we can grow and prosper.

After dinner it was time for homework. We all studied until bedtime. My aunt and uncle insist we work hard and take advantage of being Americans.

CHAPTER TEN

SUNDAY, APRIL 10
GRACIELA

We don't have to pick on Sundays, so after Mass we have time to play. I like to spend my time at the community center in town. I see many of my classmates there. I also like to see Miss Fuentes, who works at the center. She is also a student teacher at my school, and I like her a lot. She is tall and thin and graceful. She has the darkest hair and wears it pulled back from her face. Her eyes are a liquid brown, and when she smiles her white teeth seem to glow. I would like to be like her. But I am not thin at all, and my aunt cuts my hair short so I can keep it clean while I work in the fields. Miss Fuentes says I am pretty, but I think she is just being polite.

Her family also came from Mexico, but that was many years ago. It was her grandparents who moved here. They opened a restaurant, which is still successful. It is popular with white Americans who have a lot of money; it costs a lot to eat there. Both of Miss Fuentes' parents are teachers, and she will be one soon.

"*Hola*, Graciela," she greeted me. She was working at her computer while she kept an eye on the kids painting pictures or playing Ping-Pong, basketball, or soccer. The center is always busy on Sundays.

"Please call me Gracie," I asked.

"But Graciela is such a pretty name. It fits you perfectly. And please look up at me and make eye contact. You are an important person, so look people in the eyes."

"I am an American," I said. "I like to use my American name."

"America has many names," she replied. "But, OK, I'll call you Gracie. How is school going?"

"Good," I said. "I have all A's so far. I need to keep it that way so I can get a scholarship to college."

She laughed. "I have no doubt you will have many scholarship offers. You are one of the smartest kids in school."

"Thank you."

"What do you want to study in college?"

"I want to be a nurse. Nurses help people, and they are respected."

"This is so," she said. "But why not a doctor? You are smart enough, and there are many women doctors now."

"Well, I have never seen a female doctor, and I am not sure people will go to a Mexican-American woman doctor."

She laughed. "You are wise beyond your years. But times have changed, and you should be what you want to be."

"I will think about it."

"You know," she said, "doctors and nurses have the same job: to help people get and stay healthy."

"Yes," I said. "That is what I want to do."

"Good. Let me ask you a question. What do you think is the most important health problem for kids today?"

I thought for a minute. "I don't know, maybe diabetes. I have heard a lot about that recently."

"Good for you. No doubt, diabetes is a serious problem. Do you know what one of the major causes of childhood diabetes is?"

"No."

"It's obesity. Do you know what that means?"

"Being fat?" I was embarrassed because I felt fat, and I wondered if Miss Fuentes was going to tell me to lose weight.

"It's more than just fat, but you are right."

"Do you think I am fat?" I asked.

Now Miss Fuentes looked embarrassed. "I think you are very pretty," she said. "But I do think you should lose some weight because it would make you healthier."

"I don't eat that much."

"Sometimes it's not how much but what you eat. And you and I share the same problem."

"You're not fat," I said.

"No," she said, laughing. "But I have to work at it. Remember, my grandfather runs a restaurant, and his food is delicious but not always so good for you. What I meant was Mexican-Americans like you and me have a long history of eating food that can make you fat. Our culture uses a lot of inexpensive, calorie-laden foods."

"I'm not sure I really understand."

"That's OK. You will. Let me ask you a question. Have you heard of 8th Day?"

"No," I said. "Should I know it?"

"Yes, you should, and now you will. Do you think you would like to help me on something very important?"

"Yes," I said without hesitation. "Tell me more."

CHAPTER ELEVEN

SUNDAY, APRIL 17
THE MEETING

It was Sunday.

Each of the four students sat at a computer. RJ was in his bedroom while his mother worked in the kitchen. Lamar was also in his bedroom, but his Mama had gone to church, and Jeane had gone out with Rashon. Karstan sat in his room; he, too, was the only one home. Gracie was in the director's office at the center. Ms. Fuentes stood outside to make sure no one came in.

At exactly the same time, each teen turned on the computer and went to Skype. Within a minute, they heard a quiet ringing noise. A message box told them Dr. A. was calling. They all accepted the call.

The screen flickered and four boxes appeared on the screen. In three of the boxes, they saw each other. The fourth box was dark. They could see an overhead fluorescent light, as if the computer's camera was pointing toward the ceiling. It was.

"Good day," said a voice. None of the four had spoken. "You can call me Dr. A. In order to protect us all, it is important that you do not know me or know what I do. Do you understand?" RJ nodded.

The others said, "Yes." His voice was deep, so they knew he was a man, and he sounded old.

"Good. Let me introduce you to each other. Gracie, say hello and tell the boys what state you live in. Let's not use last names. The less you know about each other, the safer you will be."

The only girl on the screen was small. She had a friendly brown face and coal-black hair. A bright yellow ribbon complemented a shining, but shy, smile. "I'm Gracie, and I live in California. I am in the eighth grade, and I am here because I have some personal experience with diabetes."

The boys were silent for a while. Finally one of them spoke up.

"I'm Lamar from D...Michigan. I'm in the seventh grade." He was wiry and looked intelligent. Leaning forward in his chair made his eyes look larger.

"My name is Karstan, but call me K-man. I live in Connecticut. I'm a seventh grader, too." He kept his eyes down, as if looking for a phone to text with. His light brown hair was long and unkempt. But his impish smile implied mischief.

"I used to be from Connecticut," said RJ. "But now I live in Tennessee. Oh, and I'm RJ, and I'm an eighth grader." He sat back and looked furtively at the screen. He had green eyes and blond hair, but what the others saw first was an anxiousness they all shared.

"Welcome, all of you," said Dr. A. "You all have something in common. Someone close to you has asked you to be part of something that will help young people across the nation. I won't use the names of your contacts either. First, I want to thank you for helping. It's important work, but you can quit any time you want. No one will think less of you. It is always your choice to be a part of this mission. Second, I need to make it clear that my primary responsibility is to keep you safe and anonymous to anyone other than each other and your contacts; therefore, we have to be careful. I need your word that you will follow the rules.

"Whenever the five of us are in contact, like today, we will use Skype, which allows us to videoconference. Skype is an excellent tool and affords us a great deal of security with one exception. U.S. government agencies that exist to protect us from dangerous people have the ability to listen in on Skype conversations. However, they are only listening for certain words and phrases terrorist organizations might use. So, rule one: never use the name of this organization or our full names. We do not want the listeners confusing us with really dangerous people. We will design another format for the four of you to speak to each other. We will only use this format when I call a meeting."

"Rule number two: tell no one about your participation with 8th Day or what we are doing. I know this is hard, particularly not telling your parents."

Karstan snorted. No one seemed to notice.

"Rule number three: you must never do anything that might put you in danger. Tell your contacts—those people who asked you to be part of this—about everything you do or are about to do."

"Rule number four: I know you are curious about each other, and I know you will be talking and contacting each other, but do not reveal anything about yourselves to each other. If one of you gets caught, he cannot give up the others if he knows nothing. That's why you do not use last names, cities or towns you live in, or anything personal enough to allow someone to figure out your identities. If this sounds like I'm trying to scare you, I am. While I do not believe you are in real danger, there are people out there who are going to be very angry about what we do. And these are powerful people. Most of them are not bad people, but they are not going to like what we are doing."

"Finally, rule number five: keep your contacts aware of everything that goes on. Even if it doesn't seem important."

"Do you understand?"

Three heads nodded.

"But what if my mom figures out what's going on and wants me to tell her? Should I lie to her?" asked Lamar.

"I can't answer that for you. I would never tell you to lie. But I would also tell you that what you are doing is very important. You always have the right to quit, so if you have to decide between doing something you don't want to do or quitting, you make the choice that is right for you. No one will think less of you."

Lamar wasn't so sure.

"So, do you agree to these rules?"

Four yeses resonated.

"Good, let me give you some background. I know some of your contacts have partly filled you in on our mission, but I want you to know what we need and why. There is a battle going on right now in this country—one that most Americans don't even know about. And, yet, it is truly a battle for our survival. Never in the history of this nation has the health of our children been in such doubt. More than one half of our children are obese. We know obesity is the cause of many diseases, and we know it is a life-style choice. We can choose not to be obese. But the majority of Americans, old and young, don't even see the problem. They don't even know they are obese. The cause of obesity is simple: a combination of eating too much, making poor food choices, and not exercising.

It would seem the answer to the problem is simple: get the information in front of the adults and they will change their own and their family's eating and exercise habits. At 8th Day we are doing just that. But it's not enough. There is another enemy: the food industry, both the food suppliers and the restaurants. These companies are not evil, just lazy and profit-driven. The one and only goal is to make money, and making people fat makes money. I understand these companies. They see their only job as making money for their shareholders. At the end of the day, they give us what we want. I could not be part of that, but I do not condemn all food industry workers. They will change when we want them to.

"As long as we do not monitor nor understand what we eat, this will continue. Heavy doses of sugars of all kinds are appealing to us. It's not unlike an addiction to alcohol or cigarettes. How many of you and your parents monitor what you eat? How many check the content and calories on prepared foods? If you did, you would be amazed and appalled at how much sugar and fats are in what we eat. How many of you know how little white flour, white rice and white sugar contain nutritionally? You don't have to answer that. But because we don't pay attention, food processors, food companies and restaurants pile our food with cheap empty calories which make us fat and sick. It is time we said *No*.

"So we need to get Americans to realize they must speak up and tell the food industry that they won't stand for poor quality anymore. It won't be easy; it's not like choosing not to buy a car from a company that makes bad cars. Everybody has to eat, and there isn't a lot of competition in the food industry. In some ways it is like the car companies. Everyone knows we would be better off with cars that got great mileage and didn't pollute the air, but we have been lazy about changing because gas is still pretty cheap and a lot of people like big cars. And the automobile industry has been very slow in modifying the way they make cars, because they don't have an incentive to hurry. We do not have that luxury with the food industry. We must change soon, or it's too late for many young people in this country.

"So, where do you come in? Your contacts will talk to you about specific tasks we need you to do. Each of you has a different task we think you can handle. These are things adults cannot do as well as you can. You will be able to contact each other because as you do your own work, you will help the others organize for bigger events. I can't tell you what now because I do not know. We are setting up a Facebook site so you can communicate with each other. It will be untraceable, and you will have a phony profile that cannot be broken. You should use it to stay in touch. Lamar is our computer guy, and he will help you with IDs and other needs. OK, Lamar?"

"I guess so," he said.

"I know this was a lot for one day, so I will stop now. Your contacts will give you specific assignments. They know me, so be careful that you don't expose your contacts. If you do, it may cause them trouble and reveal who I am."

"Good luck." And then he was gone.

The group was still on, and they looked at each other.

CHAPTER TWELVE

MONDAY, APRIL 18
RJ

I was on my own.

Spring break ended, and Ryan and I had to go back to school. After listening to that guy, Dr. A., I was both excited and scared. Ryan took me for a long ride on his motorcycle. Mom told us both to wear our helmets and we did. I could tell she was sad about Ryan going back to school.

We went down to the lake where they set off the fireworks on the Fourth of July. There was a family fishing on one side, so we parked the bike and sat alone. The sun felt good.

I asked him what I should be doing. He went over what Dr. A. had said and asked if I still wanted to help.

I said, "Of course I do."

"OK, so here's your part. We believe school lunches are one of the things hurting kids the most."

"Come on," I said. "The pizza's lousy, but I don't think it will kill me."

"You might be wrong," he replied. "But that's where your work comes in. We want to know everything about school lunches and any snacks the school offers."

"I can give you our menus," I told him.

"That will be helpful, but not every school in the country serves the same food."

"We've found some of the school menus printed in local newspapers, and they look a lot alike. We could try to get the information directly from schools, but we are worried people will start asking questions about why we want it. So a menu from you helps. But it's just the start. Almost all schools get some food from the government, which means officials send memos back and forth about it. We need you to get information about the lunches and find out who determines the menu and how. We need to know who is responsible for buying the food and for setting the menus."

"Wow, sounds like a lot."

"It is. Do you think you can do it?"

"I can try."

Ryan said, "I'd like to help you, but you know much more about the way the school works than I do. Any ideas?"

"Not any good ones," I answered.

But after Ryan left, I did get an idea, or actually, the idea got me. Mr. Kohla assigned all of us a science project to work on and then present at the science fair in May. We do it every year. I never enjoyed it much, but this year I had a good reason to like it. First, I could use it to get information about the lunches, and second, I got to work with Becky. Becky belongs to the group of kids whose parents are professors at the university. She is also the smartest person in the class and maybe the prettiest. She doesn't talk to me much, none of the university kids do, but she isn't rude like some of the others. Her dad is chairman of the biology department at the university. Did I mention she's pretty? She pulls her golden hair into a ponytail most days. I could recognize her laugh anywhere, and she laughs a lot. She is a little taller than me; her height landed her the center position on the girl's basketball team. But what I notice the most are her eyes. Some kids call her Becky blue eyes.

I only see her three times a day. We both have Mr. Kohla for homeroom and for science. We also have social studies together. But Becky takes advanced English and math classes, and I don't.

The project was starting to look good.

CHAPTER THIRTEEN

TUESDAY, APRIL 19
RJ

"OK," said Mr. Kohla, "we should be ready to get started on the science projects. I am going to give you plenty of time in class to work, but some of this will have to be done out of school. I don't want to hear any complaints about whom you are working with since you picked your partner's name out of a hat. This is class, not a dance."

Some of the girls laughed.

"So," he continued, "get with your partners and choose a topic. You have forty-five minutes to do that. Then we will talk about how to set goals for your project and how to use the scientific method."

I was terrified. What if she wouldn't talk to me? What if I couldn't convince her to do the project on school lunches?

All of a sudden, she was sitting next to me. I couldn't say a word.

"I saw you with your brother on that motorcycle," she said. "He's really cute. What's his name?"

"Ryan," I managed to answer.

"And where does he go to school? He does go to college doesn't he?"

That made me mad. "Of course he does. He goes to Columbia University. It's in New York."

"I know where it is," she said. "My Dad goes there for conferences sometimes. And don't be so defensive; I didn't mean anything about it. I was just interested. I like his motorcycle."

I know I was blushing. " Well, I…think he would take you for a ride when he comes back," I stammered. "If your parents would let you."

"No problemo," she said. "My Dad had one when he was in college. He says he was born too late to be a real hippie. But he was still able to march in protest against something."

"Cool," I said. "My Grandma and Grandpa were hippies too, only a longer time ago. They got arrested once."

"That's epic," she said. "So have you thought about the project?"

"I have," I said. I think she was surprised.

"I'd like to do something on nutrition and school lunches."

"Yuck! School lunches are sooooo not good."

"Yeah," I said. "Remember the newspaper stories The Bear read in class? The ones the first lady wrote?"

"OK," said Becky.

"She talked about kids our age needing to be healthier. And remember the arguments during class? Some kids agreed and others thought she was crazy."

"Yup, some of the kids would rather eat and drink junk. They'll be sorry someday," she said. "I don't think anything will help them."

"So you don't want to do it?" I was disappointed.

"Wrong," she said. "I think it would be really great. My dad could help us, and the cafeteria witches all like me, so we could really get at the dirt."

"This was looking way too easy," I thought.

Man, was I wrong.

CHAPTER FOURTEEN

WEDNESDAY, APRIL 20
RJ

Dr. Albright was thrilled when Becky asked for his help. Apparently she had never shown interest in his work before. He gave her all sorts of stuff about nutrition and how to use the scientific method.

"This is great!" said The Bear. "I'll bet you'll learn a lot from this. And I can help by setting up time for you to talk to the cafeteria workers." He moved on to talk to another team about their project.

"Dad told me school lunches suck—what a surprise. He doesn't want me to eat them, and most days I don't," Becky said. "I'll eat the pizza, but that's about it. My dad doesn't even like the pizza. He was saying something about the USDA and food companies that I didn't really get, but he also gave me some articles and charts we can use. He has a document about school lunch regulations and child nutrition. But it's more than sixty pages long; needless to say, I didn't read it. He said it was pretty old; Congress started the lunch program way back to help kids be healthier. My dad said it was a good idea, but not many people follow the guidelines or even pay attention to them. Dad has gone to school board meetings to get some changes made, but they don't listen to him. He also said these lunches are really hurting kids and making them unhealthy."

"I eat the lunch every day," I said. "Mom doesn't usually have the time to make it for me. It's OK but not great. Ryan told me I had put on some weight since we moved here."

"Oh you're not one of those balloon kids in our class," said Becky.

I didn't think that was a very nice thing to say, but I let it go.

"Maybe not," I said, "but I am heavier than when we moved. Back home, Mom always made my lunch, and I liked it better. I also played baseball, basketball, and lacrosse. But I haven't done much here. Lacrosse was my favorite, but the school doesn't offer it."

"Probably never heard of it," said Becky.

"Can I see the stuff your dad gave you?"

"Sure. I made copies for you."

"Thanks," I said." Lets ask The Bear to get us an interview with the cafeteria ladies."

After dinner, I went to my room and pulled out the stuff Becky had given me. There was the long report, which I started to read but didn't understand. I looked at some of the articles and charts. There was one titled "My Opinion." It came from *The Tennessean*, a big newspaper in Nashville. The guy who wrote it was a professor at Vanderbilt University. He was asking why the state schools allowed soda and junk food vending machines in their buildings and why some school cafeterias had soda as a choice with lunch. He believed soda and unhealthy snacks of any kind were bad—particularly for children—and increased the risk of obesity, diabetes, and other diseases. He knew schools needed money, but he felt it was unethical to allow soda companies to sell their products in the schools. Making money from children by feeding them poison was unforgivable, he wrote. He was very angry and blamed the schools, the state, and the government bureaucrats in Washington.

If what he said was true, I couldn't understand it either. If the government set up the school lunch program to help kids, why were they hurting them? I was starting to get a little angry myself. I wanted to call Ryan but decided to wait until I learned more.

And I did learn more.

I went to Becky's house after dinner the next night. We planned to look at what we had and decide what to do. I met Dr. Albright, Becky's father. He was a short man who looked like he worked out. His hair was longer than my father's, and he wore a small earring. I think it was a diamond. He shook my hand and said to call him Woody, but I didn't think I could do that. He asked about Ryan and how he liked Columbia.

"Where are you thinking of going to college?" he asked.

"I haven't thought about it," I answered.

"Well, it's never too early. Becky tells me you are a smart guy and this project was your idea."

"Well, I guess it was."

"I think it's an ideal project, particularly here where the lunch program is unacceptable. I'm glad Mr. Kohla has been supportive. I like him too. He's different from most of the teachers at the school."

He was right about that. Mr. Kohla was much different. He listened to the kids, and he was always interesting.

"I understand he went to Williams College. A fine school."

"I didn't know that."

"So how can I help you?" he asked.

"Well," Becky said, "we have a lot of information, and it seems pretty bad, but we don't know how this works. If the government was trying to make kids healthy, how did we get lunches that are bad for us?"

"It's a good question, but complicated. It seems to me the lunch programs are more interested in making money than in keeping kids healthy. And the government is supposed to pay attention to what's going on, but they really aren't."

"But that doesn't make any sense," I said.

"No, it surely doesn't," Dr. Albright replied. "It is hard to understand, and I could teach a class full of students about this for years. But let's talk about what you can do. What you do is very important. Let me ask you some questions and make some suggestions."

He asked us what our goal was, and we told him we aimed to study the lunch program to see how healthy it was. He liked our response and discussed how scientists would find the answer.

"First," he said, "you need to gather as much information as you can. Don't start off with how bad the lunches are, even though that may be true. Start from a neutral point. For example, find out what the students who buy lunches eat every day. Then let the facts speak for themselves. Good projects always have visuals; try to create some interesting charts to show your findings. Get everything you can from your own school. Maybe you could survey kids. Maybe you can observe the students. Talk to the cafeteria people about what they think. Collect school menus and compare them to a healthy lunch. Study the nutritional value of different types of food and define what a healthy, balanced meal is. I'm sure you can find some good information online."

It was starting to make sense the way he explained it.

"I think I will have to stay away from the project though," he said. "I'm not very popular with the school or the school board because I have argued with them before about the lunches, and they didn't want to hear what I had to say. Their only issue seems to be how they can make more money for the school, which by the way is a good idea, but they need to think of other ways."

Becky's dad left, leaving the two of us at her kitchen table. We made a plan and decided who would do what. Becky took the poster work. She was going to get menus from the cafeteria and compare them to what we could find about healthy lunches. I would make up the survey and observe kids eating lunch.

But the plan changed.

CHAPTER FIFTEEN

MONDAY, APRIL 25
RJ

On Monday, when I was waiting to enter school, I saw Becky with a bunch of her girlfriends. It looked like they were laughing at me. I was embarrassed so I went and sat by the flagpole.

When the bell rang, we all went in. I was at my locker when Becky came over.

"Hey," she said.

I mumbled something.

"A problem?" she asked. "Oh, I get it. The girls were looking at you." She laughed. I was blushing again.

"They just think you're cute and were telling me I was lucky to have you as a partner."

I think I smiled.

"OK," she said. "A problem. When I told my dad the plan, he said it would probably be better if you spoke to the cafeteria witches and the secretary because they don't like him and it might change their responses. Maybe you haven't noticed, but all of us whose parents are professors aren't exactly popular with the teachers and other adults here."

"I thought you guys would be their favorites. You're the best students."

"Who knows?" But I thought she did.

So we agreed I'd get the menus and other stuff, and Becky would do the survey.

I asked The Bear if I could go to the cafeteria and office to get some things for our project, and he gave me a hall pass.

When I got to the cafeteria, the ladies were preparing for lunch. I didn't see Mrs. Nunley, who was in charge. I waited in front of the serving counter until Miss Sally noticed me and came over. She was the nicest and youngest in the cafeteria. People say she was a student at Marion County Community College and was going to be a dietitian. Everyone liked her.

"Need something, RJ?"

"Yes, ma'am. I need the week's menus and some old ones if you have any."

"What do you need them for?" she asked.

"I'm doing a science project."

"What's this all about?" Mrs. Nunley asked after overhearing my request. She had walked up behind Miss Sally. She didn't look happy, but she never did.

"RJ needs the new menu and some old ones for his science project," Miss Sally said.

"And what do you need menus for? What's this project about?"

"Not really sure yet," I replied, which wasn't exactly true. "I think we're going to survey kids to see what they like to eat." It was easy to not tell her the whole truth because I didn't like her.

"Don't know why that should be my business," she said.

"Mr. Kohla said you would have some."

"He did, did he? Well I haven't got time for this, and you can tell him that." She grabbed a piece of paper from under the counter.

"Here's this week's. I can't be wasting my time looking around for old ones. We have work to do."

"Thanks," I said and took the paper. Mrs. Nunley walked away.

"Good luck," said Miss Sally, and then she winked at me. I didn't know what the wink meant.

CHAPTER SIXTEEN

MONDAY, APRIL 25
RJ AND BECKY

It was lunchtime before I could speak to Becky alone. We sat at a table in the cafeteria by ourselves. Every so often someone from our class would come by and giggle or smirk at us. Becky gave them all "the look." That would have been enough for me.

I told her about my conversation with Mrs. Nunley.

"So what do we do now?" I asked.

She seemed serious. "Let me think," she said finally.

I did.

We ate in silence. When she picked up her apple, she looked at it and then at me.

"OK, we need to make a big move now," she said.

"Oh," I said. "What does big mean?"

"My dad always tells me to think outside of the box. So we know we want a report no one will ever forget. We know we are going to show how the lunches suck and are like poison. They don't know that. They need to think we're just dumb eighth graders who want to get an A on the project. So let's remake the project so they will be happy with us dumb kids."

I had no idea what she was talking about.

"Here's how it works. We tell Mr. Kohla Mrs. Nunley wouldn't give us any information. Then we tell him all we want to do is have a survey and a list of student favorites for our report. But we need to have the menus to be able to fill out the survey. Then we hope he goes to Mrs. Nunley or Mrs. Reardon to get the stuff. He will convince them that we are young, innocent, dumb kids."

I have to give it to her. She thought differently than anyone I knew.

That afternoon I told The Bear about my meeting with Mrs. Nunley.

"And why wouldn't she let you have the menus?"

"She said she was too busy."

"How many menus do you need?" he asked.

"Maybe two months worth," I said.

"OK, I'll talk to her."

At the end of the school day, Mr. Kohla left right away, and we figured he was going to see Mrs. Nunley. Instead of walking home, Becky and I went to the cafeteria where the kids who had to wait for their parents stayed.

We didn't go in but stood outside the doors. It wasn't long before we heard loud voices. I recognized Mr. Kohla and Mrs. Nunley. They were arguing. It didn't last long and when it stopped, Becky and I slid around the corner. Mr. Kohla came out and walked quickly up the stairway toward the office. He didn't see us.

"Ouch," said Becky. "Mr. Kohla really got it from the head witch."

"What will we do if we can't get the menus?"

"Don't worry," said Becky. " I don't think The Bear is done."

And he wasn't.

CHAPTER SEVENTEEN

TUESDAY, APRIL 26
RJ AND BECKY

When I got to school the next day, Becky was waiting at my locker.

"Let's see how well The Bear roared," she said.

We went into the room and put our books on our desks.

"Becky and RJ, I need to talk with you," said Mr. Kohla. "In the hall, please."

Becky gave me a little smile as we walked into the hall. Mr. Kohla looked serious.

"You are going to get the lunch menus for the last two months," he said. "But I need to ask you some questions."

"Go ahead," said Becky.

"I know the formal plan for the project isn't due until Friday, but tell me now what you are trying to do with your project."

I think I started to turn red. No way could I talk, but Becky wasn't bothered.

"Well, we're not totally sure," she said. "But mostly we want to find out what the kids in the eighth grade eat when they buy their lunches. We remembered the stuff we discussed about the first lady's ideas about school lunches, and we wondered what our students were eating of all the healthy choices offered in the cafeteria."

I almost gagged.

"We figured we'd survey kids and find out what they like and don't like on the menus. Later, we will watch what they eat and see if they are making good choices. Then we could make this ginormous display listing everything and showing our results."

The Bear looked at her with serious eyes; she was smiling.

"So RJ," he asked, "is that about right?" He was talking to me but still looking at Becky.

" Well…yeah. Yes. That sounds right." I managed to reply.

So now I was lying.

"All right, then. I'll have the menus after lunch."

CHAPTER EIGHTEEN

TUESDAY, APRIL 26
RJ AND BECKY

I was glad I had brought my lunch. I didn't want to see Mrs. Nunley in the lunch line. Whenever I looked at the serving line, I was sure she was staring at me. Becky came over and sat down.

"The head witch sends her love," she said.

"Becky, what is going to happen when Mr. Kohla finds out our project isn't just about what kids like?"

"Worry about that later," she said. "He's one of the good guys. He might be angry for a while, but he'll get over it."

"But we lied to him," I said.

"Well not exactly. We can always say that when we were doing our research, we discovered other things. Besides, he'll get over it."

"But what if he gets in trouble with Mrs. Reardon?"

"Duh, haven't you heard of tenure? They can't fire him. Besides, if we keep him in the dark, then he really isn't responsible for what we do."

I was worried that Becky actually made some sense. What was happening to me?

Our last class of the day was science with Mr. Kohla. While we were getting settled, Miss Sally walked into the class. She was still wearing her cafeteria stuff: apron and hairnet. She gave Mr. Kohla an envelope. When she left, she looked at me and I thought she winked again.

Mr. Kohla came over and handed me the envelope. I put it in one of my folders.

I don't remember much about the class because I was thinking about what we were going to do with those menus. The bell rang and the halls filled up with kids going to their lockers. I opened up the folder and saw several menus. The first looked like this month's.

MIDDLE SCHOOL MENU

BLALOCK MIDDLE SCHOOL

	MONDAY	TUESDAY	WEDNESDAY	THURSDAY	FRIDAY
1	**2** CORN DOG / FRENCH FRIES / APPLE SAUCE / SALAD / COOKIES / FRUIT PIE — MILK	**3** HAM HOAGIE / FRENCH FRIES / APPLE SAUCE / SALAD / COOKIES / FRUIT TURNOVER — MILK	**4** BAR-B-Q CHICKEN / FRENCH FRIES / APPLE SAUCE / SALAD / COOKIES / FRUIT POP — MILK	**5** NO SCHOOL	**6** PIZZA / TATERS / APPLE SAUCE / SALAD / COOKIES / FRUIT POP — MILK
2	**9** HAM/CHEESE / CHEESE BROCCOLI / APPLE SAUCE / SALAD / COOKIES / FRUIT PIE — MILK	**10** CHICKEN / FRENCH FRIES / APPLE SAUCE / SALAD / COOKIES / FRUIT TURNOVER — MILK	**11** RIB SANDWICH / FRENCH FRIES / APPLE SAUCE / SALAD / COOKIES / FRUIT POP — MILK	**12** CHEESE STICKS / FRENCH FRIES / APPLE SAUCE / SALAD / COOKIES / FRUIT POP — MILK	**13** PIZZA / TATERS / APPLE SAUCE / SALAD / COOKIES / FRUIT POP — MILK
3	**16** CHICKEN POT PIE / CHEESE BROCCOLI / CHEESEY GREEN BEANS / SALAD / COOKIES / APPLE PIE — MILK	**17** BURRITO / CREAM CORN / CHEESEY GREEN BEANS / SALAD / COOKIES / APPLE PIE — MILK	**18** GRILLED CHEESE / FRIED ONION RINGS / CHEESEY GREEN BEANS / SALAD / COOKIES / APPLE PIE — MILK	**19** SPAGHETTI/MEAT SAUCE / SUGAR GLAZED CARROTS / CHEESEY GREEN BEANS / SALAD / COOKIES / APPLE PIE — MILK	**20** PIZZA / TATERS / CHEESEY GREEN BEANS / SALAD / COOKIES / APPLE PIE — MILK
4	**23** CHICKEN NUGGETS / FRENCH FRIES / CHEESEY GREEN BEANS / SALAD / COOKIES / FRUIT PIE — MILK	**24** TURKEY NUGGET / FRENCH FRIES / CHEESEY GREEN BEANS / SALAD / COOKIES / FRUIT PIE — MILK	**25** CORN DOG / FRENCH FRIES / CHEESEY GREEN BEANS / SALAD / COOKIES / FRUIT PIE — MILK	**26** CHEESE TACO / FRENCH FRIES / CHEESEY GREEN BEANS / SALAD / COOKIES / FRUIT PIE — MILK	**27** PIZZA / FRENCH FRIES / CHEESEY GREEN BEANS / SALAD / COOKIES / FRUIT PIE — MILK
5	**30** CORN DOG / FRENCH FRIES / CREAM CORN / SALAD / COOKIES / APPLE PIE — MILK	**31** HAM HOAGIE / FRENCH FRIES / CREAM CORN / SALAD / COOKIES / APPLE PIE — MILK			

I grabbed my stuff and was about to walk home when someone hit me with a notebook.

"Ouch," I said, turning around. Becky was holding a piece of paper folded in half.

"This is epic," she said. She looked absolutely surprised. I had never seen that look. "Come with me."

The school is on Phillips Street near Blalock Road, which was a four-lane road connecting the town of Blalock and the university with the small town of Weaver just a few miles away. The university was away from the main road. It was about a half mile up Phillips. The houses on Phillips Street were mostly professors' homes or offices for the university. The third house up the road was Becky's. It was much bigger than mine and had a large front porch. It was two stories painted yellow and white. The yard was large with lots of flowers. In the back I saw a small, open round building with ivy growing up the sides. Becky told me it was a gazebo. She went right to it and sat on the floor.

"What's this about?" I asked. I was puffing a little from running after her.

"Shhhh," she quieted me. "Let me finish." I waited as she read whatever was on the paper she had in her hand. When she stopped, she just looked out at the yard.

"This is just too good," she said.

"What is?"

"Look for yourself. I found this in my locker." She handed me the paper.

The paper was a typed note.

Don't worry about who I am. Just read this and do whatever you want with it.

Mrs. Nunley has her desk in the cafeteria office. She keeps a lot of papers in the top right-hand drawer. Most of them are menus and menu suggestions, but there are also e-mails from the school board and a bunch of rules and regulations from the State and U.S. government about the school lunch program. There is a copier in the office. It has no key number, so anyone can use it.

Mrs. Nunley's computer is on the desk. Her user ID is top-chef, and her password is potatochip. In the document section, you will find memos about lunches from important people. Use what you can. Do not to try to find me.
TGW

"What is TGW?" I asked.

"Dunno, maybe it's a hint about who gave this to us. Doesn't matter," Becky said.

"I don't think I like this," I replied.

"Don't be stupid," said Becky. "This is our chance to really do some good stuff with our project."

"But what if we get caught? My mom would kill me. Maybe we should tell your dad?"

"Noooo way. He wants to help us, but he would consider this stealing and wouldn't allow it."

"But it is stealing," I protested.

"Not exactly," she said. "After all, someone gave this to us. We didn't steal it. So someone wants us to know what's in there, and I want to find out what."

"I don't know," I said. "I need to think."

"Don't think too long or I'll be looking for another partner."

I went home.

CHAPTER NINETEEN

TUESDAY, APRIL 26
RJ AND BECKY

That night I couldn't think; I felt so confused. I knew this project was important; but now that lying and maybe stealing had become part of the plan, I didn't know what to do. I was mixed up. Should I do what my brother and Becky and all the other people at 8th Day wanted or fink out? I was afraid of what might happen. Mom already seemed unhappy and stressed; it wouldn't help the situation if I got caught. I could get suspended, or even arrested. None of that sounded good. I didn't want to get paddled or anything else, but upsetting mom scared me more. So I called Ryan.

"What's up big guy?" he asked.

"I need help," I said. "You know that thing we talked about?"

"Yes," he answered, sounding concerned. " But let's not use any names here."

"OK. Stuff is happening, some of it good, some maybe not," I said.

"Explain."

"Well, I am doing a report at school focusing on what we talked about."

"That's good," he said.

"I know. I know. But we, my partner and me, are about to get some things that someone else has and they don't want us to have them and they don't know we will get them," I said. I hoped he understood what I was saying.

"I see," he said.

"Do you?"

" I think so. You are worried about getting into trouble."

"Yeah," I said. "But also about mom."

Ryan didn't say anything for what seemed like a long time.

"Will this stuff be helpful? Is it really important?" he asked.

I had to think. "Yes," I said. "I think so."

"Remember what I told you that you can always do?" he asked.

"I remember."

"Well," he said, "then we are where I thought we might be. And here's the deal. You have to make the choice. I'm not going to; I can't tell you what to do. But I can tell you this is only the beginning. I understand these things are not what you would like to do or would ever do unless there was a really good reason. So you need to decide if this is worth the risk. In the end, if you're in, you're in; if you're out, you're out. Regardless of your decision, you will always be number one to me, always the best brother in the world. I wish I could help, but this is your call."

We were both silent for a while.

"OK," I said. "I will think some more. Thanks for talking to me. It helped."

"I hope so, big guy." Then we hung up.

I didn't get much sleep, but when I left for school the next morning, I knew.

CHAPTER TWENTY

WEDNESDAY, APRIL 27
RJ AND BECKY

Becky was waiting by my locker.

"Well?" she asked.

"I spent the night thinking about it, and I made a decision."

"In, out? Let's get cracking," she said.

"What?" I didn't know what she was talking about.

"It's from a movie, an old movie called *West Side Story*. Don't you know anything?" She looked exasperated, but then she smiled. "Just kidding. It means are you in or not."

"I'm in," I said.

"Good. I knew I could count on you." She smiled at me again. I liked her smile. It made me feel like I was doing the right thing. "We can't talk until lunch. After we eat let's go outside and make some plans."

We went way back on the playground. No one was near us. One of Becky's friends started to walk over, but Becky waved her away. It was warm for April, and we sat in the shade of an old tree. There were carvings on the tree, probably from the university students.

"I showed all the menus to my father. He read them and groaned. He told me they didn't look bad on paper, but we need to find out more about what the kids choose to eat and what the cafeteria offers that isn't listed on the menu. I told him we were going to do a survey, watch the kids' eating habits, and keep notes about what they really ate."

"OK," I said. "We can do that. That's what Mr. Kohla is expecting anyway."

"I didn't want to tell my dad we plan to collect and add things that would tell people how bad the lunches really are. If I did, he might have tried to talk me out of it. He's sure the people who run the school don't like him, or me, or most of the families from the university."

"Do you think that, too?" I asked.

"I don't know, but I don't care either," she said. "But now we have to figure out how to get the dirt on the ptomaine palace. Any ideas?"

I was surprised she asked me, but I had an answer. "Yeah, I've been working on that. The note told us where to find the information. Someone is trying to hand it to us. So we need to go get it."

"I got that part," she said. "But how do we get it? The witch is not inviting us into the gingerbread house."

"I know," I replied. "But whoever sent the note knows that too, so there must be some time and way to get in. Here's what I think. The cafeteria closes after lunch. You can hear them cleaning up during the afternoon if you walk by. It seems to me that by two o'clock it's quiet in there. And I have noticed the ladies go to their cars around then. You can see the parking lot behind the cafeteria from our social studies classroom. But Mrs. Nunley doesn't leave with the others. I guess she has to work a little longer. But when we leave school, her car is gone too. She drives an awful-looking, old pickup that makes loud noises and belches black smoke. I see her pulling in during the morning."

"OK, OK, so what do we do?" she asked.

"Patience," I said.

"Who are you, Master Po?"

"What?"

"Never mind," she said, "it's from an old TV show. Let's hear your plan."

"The after-school program ends at four thirty, and the place clears out quickly. Usually everyone, including Mrs. Reardon and the office staff, are gone by five. But the janitors stay to clean. We need to spend a few days studying where they work at what time. I think we should watch on different days, so they don't see us together."

"Beastly," she said, clearly excited. "I never knew you were so devious."

I think that was supposed to be a compliment.

"OK, when we know their schedule, we enter through the gym door, which is always open, and we head for the cafeteria. If anyone sees us, we will tell him we need books from our lockers. Then we get to the cafeteria and into the office. We need to get the papers and copy them, then turn on the computer and log in so we can check the documents."

"I bet I can do that," she said. "I'll have my dad show me just in case. He loves it when I ask for help. But how do we know the doors to the cafeteria and the witch's office will be open?"

"I thought about that," I replied. "But whoever sent the note would know, and I'm guessing we'll be able to get in."

The bell rang, and we walked back to class.

CHAPTER TWENTY-ONE

TUESDAY, MAY 3
RJ AND BECKY

After four days of watching, we had the custodians' schedules down. There was only one janitor after school. The daytime custodian, Mr. Ladd, left when he finished cleaning the cafeteria after the last lunch. The other custodian, Mr. Simpson, came to work at noon and stayed until eight o'clock. After school, Mr. Simpson started cleaning all areas except the classrooms. He worked on those after the teachers left. He cleaned the office area of the cafeteria as soon as all the kids who waited for their rides in the cafeteria had gone. So we decided to make our move at five o'clock. By then Mr. Simpson was cleaning the sixth-grade wing, which was the farthest away from the cafeteria.

It was Friday, so everyone left earlier than usual. We left school at the regular time, and I walked over to Becky's. I told mom I was going to Becky's, and she thought it was a good idea. She had to clean up after working at the university and get to Shenanigan's by five thirty.

Becky and I sat in the gazebo.

"Should we wear masks?" Becky said.

"Don't make jokes," I said. "This is serious and we need to be careful."

"Oh, stop worrying," she said. "What's the worst that could happen?"

"I don't want to think about that."

"All right," she said. "Let's go."

We had talked all week about how this would work. We would enter through the gymnasium. We had our book bags over our shoulders. If anyone saw us, we would claim we forgot stuff we needed for homework and had to go to our lockers.

The gym door was closed but not locked. There was a stone holding it open. We had seen Mr. Simpson smoke cigarettes by that door, but not until later. The gym was empty and our footsteps sounded like loud smacks on the floor. I tried to walk silently. Becky didn't seem to notice. Out of the gym, we went in to the hallway. We turned left and went by the offices. No lights were on. The cafeteria was at the end of the corridor, which had a wall of windows that looked out on the courtyard. The seventh and eighth grade classrooms were on either sides of the courtyard. If someone had been in a classroom, we could have been seen. But no one was. Mr. Simpson was in the sixth-grade wing.

We went out the main entry to the cafeteria. It smelled like wax and bleach. We walked along the wall to the door that went into the cooking and serving area. Becky tried the door slowly so as not to make a sound.

"Crap," she said. "It's locked."

We hadn't counted on this.

"I don't get it," she said. "The note made it sound like we could get in the office. What was TGW thinking?"

"Wait a minute," I said, "maybe we're not thinking. There's a door in the back of the kitchen; let's try that one. We slowly retreated through the front doors and walked down the hallway. We kept an eye on the classrooms to make sure no one was watching us. We turned the corner, which lead to an area used as a loading zone for the school. There was a metal door that rolled up to the top when the door was open; it was big enough for a truck to back up to it. The whole area smelled of sour milk. There were still-full garbage cans at the far end of the big room. On the left, as we turned the corner, we saw the door leading to the kitchen. It was metal and had scratches and dents from loading and unloading. Becky reached out to turn the handle. She grabbed it and looked at me. She didn't seem as confident now. The handle turned. She looked at me and smiled. She pulled on the door, and it groaned and screeched. We both jumped and Becky almost let go of the handle. We both looked around and listened for the sound of footsteps, but there were none. Becky still held on to the handle. She took a deep breath and kept pulling. It made less noise, or seemed to. When it was open far enough, we both slid in sideways making ourselves as skinny as possible. Inside, it was dark. We were in the back of the kitchen. There was enough light to see reasonably. Becky started to pull the door closed, and I looked at her and put my finger to my lips. She slowly closed the door. It made a clunk as it finally shut.

"It's dark," I said.

"We can stop for a minute and our eyes will adjust," said Becky. "But, just in case." She reached in her backpack and pulled out a pen.

"What is…" I started to ask.

She touched the pen and a beam of light shone. It was not much, but it helped us see three or four feet ahead.

"Oh," I said.

By now my eyes had adjusted enough that I could see the blackened stoves and ovens hulking to our left and the beaten up wooden table sitting in the center of the long, rectangular room. We both looked around and then moved slowly, keeping away from the things that would make noise if we touched them. Now I could see knives, forks, and long-handled spoons hanging overhead. Becky had the pen on, pointed in front of us. When we came to the end of the stoves, we could see another door, wooden this time. When we reached it, Becky motioned for me to open it. I grabbed the handle and immediately started worrying about fingerprints. But I turned the doorknob.

"It's unlocked," I said.

Becky shushed me. The door opened inward, so I pushed slowly. Becky nudged me out of the way and pointed to the light inside. We were facing a scarred wooden desk. It looked like it had been a teacher's desk once. There was a wooden chair on the other side. We saw pens and papers, a phone, and a computer on the desk. What looked like a printer/copier sat behind it. There was an empty wastepaper basket next to the copier. None of the machines had any lights on. When I closed the door behind us, it was very dark inside the office. I could only see what Becky shined the light on. She was moving it around the room, which was pretty barren. No pictures or decorations. There was a big magnetic board with days, times, and names on it. I guessed it was for the cafeteria workers. It smelled like smoke inside, which surprised me because no smoking is allowed in the building or on the grounds. I knew the custodians smoked but always outside in a doorway. Becky walked around the desk. A long drawer ran from the left corner for about two thirds the length of the desk. Three larger drawers lined the right side. Becky pulled at the long drawer, but it didn't open.

"The note said the right drawer," I whispered.

"I know, I know," she said, sounding annoyed. "I'm just curious."

She opened the top-right drawer. It held paper clips, pens, rubber bands, and pushpins, and most importantly, a pile of papers. Becky pulled them out, placing them on the desk. We found notes, printed, e-mails, letters, and memos. Becky started separating them into two piles.

"These we will copy," she said pointing to the stack on the left, "and these we won't."

"How do we know what to keep?" I asked.

"I'm not really sure," she said, "but I am keeping anything that is to or from the state or federal government and anything that has an important heading on it. Like this one."

She held one up. The top read State Board of Education, Nashville, TN.

"That makes sense," I said.

"Here," she said. "As I put them in the pile, you go over there and make a copy of each one. She pointed her light to the copier. Touch the on button and you will have enough light to work."

I did what she told me. I set the first paper face down and made a copy. It looked fine. I made separate piles for the originals and the copies. When I finished with what I had, I took the originals back to Becky and picked up the last batch. I went back to work at the copier and then heard the computer come on.

"Push mute," I said.

"OK, OK."

When I finished, I carried the papers to the desk. Becky had logged on using the ID and password we read in the note. She was in the document section and looking at some files.

"There are too many," she said. "And I can't decide which ones we need. This isn't going to work."

"We *need* to get out of here," I said. "We're pushing our luck." Her shoulders slumped, but I knew she agreed. She shut the computer down, and we put the papers back in the desk and loaded the copies into her backpack.

CHAPTER TWENTY-TWO

TUESDAY, MAY 3
RJ AND BECKY

We backed our way out of the office and passed by the ovens and stoves again. We heard a loud noise and froze. I didn't breathe. Everything was quiet and then another noise echoed through the room.

"It's the custodian emptying the garbage from the loading area," Becky said.

"We need to get out of here," I replied, feeling an urgency to run.

"Yes, but quietly."

"Wait," I said, "we can't go back the way we came. He'll see us."

"No," said Becky. "We're going out through the cafeteria."

"But the door is locked!" I think I was starting to panic.

"It locks from the inside," she said. "We'll go out and lock it behind us."

I didn't know if she was right or not, but I didn't have a better plan. Step by quiet step we made our way toward the door of the cafeteria. As we turned, I slipped on the floor, which was still a little wet from mopping earlier in the day. My sneaker jammed against the wall and made a slight bumping sound. Something was about to come out of my mouth when Becky's hand covered it. I could hardly see her in the darkness, but it didn't feel like she was smiling. We stood still.

"Who's there?" It was the voice of the custodian. My heart stopped. Becky kept her hand over my mouth. Nothing but silence for what seemed forever. Then we heard the noises of the garbage cans again. Becky took her hand off my mouth, and we worked our way to the door. Becky grabbed the handle, turned the lock, and opened the door. The brightness in the cafeteria blinded me for a second. Becky pointed to me and to the door. I walked into the cafeteria. Becky relocked the door and closed it quietly. As quickly and silently as we could, we walked through the cafeteria and through the big doors into the hallway. The door closed without a sound. I realized I hadn't taken a breath since the janitor called out. I inhaled. We were safe.

CHAPTER TWENTY-THREE

TUESDAY, MAY 3
RJ AND BECKY

Halfway down the hallway, I started to relax.

"Hey, you kids, stop right there."

Caught. It was the custodian. He was at the cafeteria door and looking right at us. I was getting ready to run, but Becky touched my hand.

"Are you talking to us, sir?" Becky asked.

"Don't be wise with me," he replied. "Do you see anyone else?"

Becky made a point of looking around and then shrugged her shoulders.

"No, I guess not."

"Come here," he said, pointing at the ground in front of him. My heart was pounding.

Becky started walking toward him, but I couldn't move. She turned around and looked at me as if to say, *What choice do we have?* The custodian leaned his broom against the wall as we reached him.

"Yes, sir?" Becky asked.

"What are you kids doing here? You're not supposed to be in school at this time."

"Well, I have this project I need to do, and I left stuff in my locker. RJ was with me, so we came over to get what I needed."

"So what were you doing in the cafeteria?"

"Cafeteria? I just told you that I needed to go to my locker."

"Yeah, I heard you, but I know you were in the cafeteria."

My mouth was dry. I knew if I had to talk I wouldn't be able to.

"Why would we want to be in the smelly cafeteria?" Becky asked.

"I don't know. You tell me."

"You're not making any sense," said Becky.

"Now don't talk back to me."

"I'm not talking back. I'm answering your questions."

"I don't believe you, and I'm going to tell the principal."

"Go right ahead. I'm Becky Albright and this is RJ Johnson. And what is your name? I want to be able to tell my dad who you are."

"Don't threaten me. I'll tell Mrs. Reardon you were rude, and she'll punish both of you."

"Not in your lifetime," Becky said. "My dad will not let that happen."

I wanted to tell her to stop talking, but I didn't know what to say.

"So, we're out of here." She turned and grabbed my arm, and we kept moving.

"This ain't over. You two brats are going to be in trouble."

Becky turned. "Brats?" she said. " My dad will really love to hear that."

We kept walking until we were back at the gazebo. Becky was finally quiet.

"Now we are in trouble," I said.

"Forget it," she said. "Nothing is going to happen."

"Nothing? You just lied to him."

"Didn't," she said.

"Whaaa?" I stammered.

"I never told him we weren't in the cafeteria. I just asked him why he thought we were."

"But it's the same thing."

"No, no," she said. "Not at all. Now let's look at this stuff and decide what we need to do next. I have a great place to hide these papers."

I didn't know what to say.

CHAPTER TWENTY-FOUR

FRIDAY, APRIL 22
GRACIELA

It had been two weeks since Miss Fuentes had talked to me about 8th Day. I wondered what the other people I had met on the Internet were doing, but I knew I was not supposed to talk about it. Since we spoke, I had spent time checking out information about weight and diet, mostly online but also from some articles and books that Miss Fuentes gave to me.

I understand now the difference between the types of food a person chooses to eat and how much she eats. Miss Fuentes told me it's not always the amount of food a person eats but what she eats that can lead to weight gain, and many Mexican-Americans are overweight and have more diseases because of their eating habits. I didn't want to be fat. The boys in my class make fun of the girls who are overweight, and I don't like it. So this information was important to me.

The Centers for Disease Control (CDC) website said Hispanic children have a 21 percent higher obesity rate than Anglos. And obese children are being diagnosed with type 2 diabetes. That really scared me! My mom had diabetes, and the report said the disease often runs in families.

So now that I know all these things, I have tried to change my eating habits. I live in a wonderful part of the country because we have fresh fruit and vegetables all year long. My Aunt Belinda is a wonderful cook, but many of her meals have too much fat, which can cause weight gain. I have shared with her some of the things I have read about healthy eating. It was Friday night and I had little homework, so I asked to help her in the kitchen.

"You think you are a cook now?" she asked me with a smile.

"No," I said, "but I would like to learn."

"Are you going to tell me what we should be eating?" she looked at me suspiciously.

"Certainly not," I said. "But I would like to share some of the things I have learned from Miss Fuentes and from the websites that I have visited."

"Ahhh, Miss Fuentes again. She is a lovely person and so smart, but I don't want her making you forget who you are."

"She would never do that. She believes we should feel proud to be Mexican-Americans. And remember her family is in the restaurant business, so she knows some things about food."

"Well, I agree with her about being proud of who we are."

"I am proud, Aunt Belinda, but today I read how Mexican-Americans are fatter and have more diabetes than Anglos."

"What do you mean?" Aunt Belinda asked.

"Much of our food is very good. We eat some fruits and vegetables and lots of beans. But some of our food is cooked with fats that are bad for us. Your tasty *rajas* are made with cream and the *empanadas* are fried. The corn in your delicious *esquites* is very good, but all that butter is not."

"Well, don't you know a great deal," she said. Then she laughed. "But I have cooked like this for many years. What will my recipes taste like if we don't use cream and butter, and if we don't fry the *empanadas?*"

"Miss Fuentes has given me recipes with substitutions for the cream, butter, and frying. She says they are just as tasty. The recipes show how you can use low-fat milk or low-fat yogurt instead of cream, and you can use olive oil instead of butter and lard. She says we should eat lots of fruits and vegetables and high-fiber foods like nuts and beans. We should drink milk and water instead of soda and other sugary drinks."

"Oh, so many ideas. You are very smart Graciela, and maybe we should try some of these new things. After all this is a new life for all of us."

So Aunt Belinda started using some of the recipes and preparations that Miss Fuentes gave me. I helped her in the kitchen whenever I could. Some of the boys complained at first, but soon they were eating everything new my aunt made. My uncle made it easy, declaring new lands require new traditions.

Even after a week of the new meals, I began to feel better. I had more energy, and I was losing some weight. But I still had a problem I wanted to talk to Miss Fuentes about.

But because of all the good cooking I was getting at home, it was hard to eat the lunches at school. They always served overcooked meat and vegetables with french fries and lots of sweets like pies and cookies. I thought about 8th Day and was glad to be a part of it, even if it only helped my home for now.

CHAPTER TWENTY-FIVE

SATURDAY, APRIL 23
GRACIELA

When I went to the center the next day, Miss Fuentes asked to speak to me alone. We went for a walk in the beautiful sunshine. It was clear and clean. The little wooden houses where the workers and their families lived were scrubbed clean, and people were outside sweeping their porches, tending their gardens, and visiting. We walked away from the center to a small, fenced park. It was shaded and had swings and slides for the little kids. Children were playing everywhere.

We sat on a bench, watching the children.

"Miss Fuentes, I wanted you to know that my aunt has been cooking healthier meals, and I am feeling more energy already."

"That's great, Gracie."

"Even the boys have decided they like the new cooking."

"Wow, that's saying something!" Miss Fuentes said. "Gracie, I want to talk to you about 8th Day. Are you still willing to help?"

"Oh, yes," I said, "more than ever."

"Well, we need you now. I will help, of course, and remember if anything happens, I will take the responsibility. But if you can do this, it keeps 8th Day protected."

"What is it?"

"We need you to start a web page. The page will be for kids your age and will include information about staying healthy. We would like to call it BFFKids. You would be the Webmaster, but we would set it up so no one would know it was you."

"That sounds like fun. It certainly doesn't sound dangerous."

"Well," she replied, "it shouldn't be, but we plan to post things, particularly about school lunches, that some people will not like. On the other hand, because it's a kid's site, we don't think too many people will pay attention."

"Sounds like fun to me. When do we start?" I asked.

"How about today?"

"Let's do it!"

"Good, let's go back to my office. I have started to set up the site, and I want you to help. When it's ready, we will launch with information about childhood obesity and what diet has to do with that. Then we will start adding more information, specifically about school lunches. After that we have a bigger plan that you are going to have to do by yourself," Miss Fuentes said.

"What is it?" I asked.

"Let's wait until we get closer, and I will explain it all to you."

"Miss Fuentes, can I ask you a question?"

"Of course," she answered.

"Lately I haven't been feeling really good. Sometimes while working in the fields, I get dizzy and have to sit down. I sit where no one will see me. Sometimes when I'm doing my homework, I can't see very well. My eyes don't see anything. It goes away, but it scares me."

Miss Fuentes took my hands and looked in my eyes.

"What did your aunt say?" she asked.

"I didn't say anything to her because I didn't want to worry her. She has so many of us to take care of. I did look on the Internet, however, and learned that diabetes runs in families. My mother had this disease. It also said that 95 percent of people with diabetes are obese. I am not obese, although I need to lose some weight, but I am afraid I might be getting this disease. I felt better, though, when I read many people live long and healthy lives if they take care of themselves by eating good food and getting plenty of exercise."

"Well, I think you should definitely see a doctor, just to see what it might have been."

"I don't want to worry my aunt."

"I can understand that, but this is important."

"Isn't there something I can do first?" I asked.

"Well," she answered, "you have already started by talking to your aunt about cooking and making some healthy changes. We plan to post a MyPlate picture on BFFKids to show kids what to eat. Your plate should have mostly vegetables and fruits and more grain than protein. Do you know what grains and proteins are?"

"Yes, I think so. Grains are things like wheat, corn, rice, and oats. Proteins are meats, fish, eggs, and beans."

"Exactly," said Miss Fuentes. "Start by trying to follow the MyPlate picture, and be sure to drink milk or water, never soda. Try to limit cookies, pies, and ice cream. Tell me what you do for exercise."

"Well, I work in the fields and I walk to and from school each day."

"Working in the fields is hard work, Gracie, but it is not cardiovascular exercise. That's the kind that keeps your heart strong. You can get that if you walk fast enough on the way to school."

"How do I know if I'm walking fast enough?"

"Try talking when you walk. If you need to take a breath between words, you are walking for exercise." Miss Fuentes showed me. "Hi (breath) Graciela (breath). How (breath) are (breath) you (breath)?"

She sounded funny, but I said I would try to walk faster. I also promised to work on my eating. "Eating healthy will be very hard at school," I told Miss Fuentes.

"Yes, that is true, Gracie. The BFFKids website will be very help- ful for you and other children who eat school lunches."

"I also found a site called diabetes.org. It had so much informa- tion. That's where I saw that dizziness and eye problems could be a sign of diabetes. I learned that when I eat my body turns the food into a sugar called glucose. I get energy from this glucose, but if I have diabetes my body does not make something called insulin, which the glucose needs to give me energy. That is why people with diabetes have to give themselves insulin shots. I don't want to do that. Miss Fuentes, I don't understand all of this. Can you help?"

"Remember," Miss Fuentes said, "whatever I tell you is no substi- tute for what a doctor knows, and he or she can tell you what you need to do. Promise me you will see one soon. But eating healthy and exercising are always good things."

"I will," I vowed.

We went back to her office, and she showed me the plans for the site and some of the ideas she wanted to include. She asked me to give her advice on what kids would like to know and how to put it in their language. It was great fun, and I felt like I was doing something important.

But I was curious about what I would have to do later. I wanted to tell my aunt, but I knew I couldn't. She would worry, and that wouldn't be fair. Besides, none of this was anything that should upset anyone.

CHAPTER TWENTY-SIX

FRIDAY, APRIL 22
LAMAR

After the talk with Dr. A. and the other three members of the group, I expected to have something to do right away. But after a week, I hadn't heard anything, so I thought I should talk to Rashon. He brought Jeane home from school on Friday, and they were planning on going to a movie. Mama was still at work, so I could talk to him alone.

"Rashon, I haven't heard anything, so I don't know what I should be doing."

"Don't worry, Lamar," he said. "Things take time. Right now one of the other members is doing work you will have to help him with."

"But, I'm ready," I said. "And I'm not real good at waiting."

"Well, you will need to learn. And you need to be ready when you are needed. Have you set up the Facebook accounts?"

"No," I replied. "I was waiting for a go-ahead."

"Well here's the deal, Lamar, you have to learn to anticipate. There is no reason those accounts can't be set up now. In fact, do it as soon as you can, and then give me the names for their dummy accounts. I will see that they get distributed to the members of your team. And when the time comes, you will be able to speak to each other. Remember, though, you should only talk to them when absolutely necessary. And check it out with me or Jeane."

I went ahead and set up the accounts. I have my real account, of course, but I set up a phony one for myself. I named my alias Luke; he's a thirty-five-year-old man who works for a publishing company in Philadelphia. He's married and has two kids. I made up a lot more stuff. Then I created one for RJ, Gracie, and Karstan. They were all very different. I set up their IDs and passwords, too.

It was pathetically simple. Even Jeane and Rashon don't understand how much I know and can do with a computer. I have a friend at school who can play five instruments already, and she's really good. I asked her one time how she learned so many so fast. She said she really didn't know; she just heard the music in her head and could play it right away. After she got a little help on each of the instruments, she was ready to go. She says it's a gift. Of course, she practices and studies all the time, too, but she loves music.

I guess that's like me and computers. Right away, I just seemed to know how they worked and what they could do. I was also lucky to have Ms. Carson in the fourth grade; she encouraged me and taught me things I needed to know. Plus she showed me magazines about computing, and I started reading them all, as many as I could get. Then I learned how to use the Internet. I still visit sites where I can chat with other people who are good with computers, and we all share what we know with each other.

I was still up when Rashon and Jeane got back from the movie. Mama was in bed, and I think they were kissing when I called out.

"What are you doing still up?" asked Jeane.

I don't think she was angry but maybe a little embarrassed that I knew they had been kissing.

"I need to show you guys some stuff." They came into my room.

"Here I want you to see the accounts."

"You mean you finished them already?" Rashon asked.

"No time at all."

"Wow. Let me see."

I showed them.

"That is amazing," said Jeane. "I knew you were good, but not how good."

I smiled. "Really, it was easy."

"Give me all of the IDs and passwords and anything else I will need," Rashon said. "I will get them to the people who will get them to your group."

Now we were connected.

CHAPTER TWENTY-SEVEN

TUESDAY, MAY 3
RJ AND BECKY

"There seem to be two kind of papers," said Becky. "Two are about the soda and vending machines in school. The others congratulate the cafeteria staff for increases in income due to food selection. Here you look."

She handed me the pile.

Blalock School Lunch Administrator
Mrs. Nunley
Blalock, TN 37555

Dear Mrs. Nunley,

Congratulations. Blalock Middle School has exceeded expectations for this year's annual income. Your expertise in utilizing over 85% of foods provided by the USDA's Child Nutrition Commodity Program saved the school district thousands of dollars. Your food preparation choices such as cookies serving as a grain and French fries serving as a vegetable have increased income by over 35%; your ability to minimize food choices and maximize food reutilization has decreased costs by almost 50%.

Again, congratulations on your excellent performance in increasing this year's annual school nutrition income.

Sincerely,
Angela Michaels, Director
TN Nutrition Board
Administration Building
1100 Middle School Avenue
Nashville, TN 37243-0389
Phone:(555)555-5555 or 1-800-555-FOOD

Cc: Mrs. Reardon

TN Nutrition Board

Blalock School Lunch Administrator
Mrs. Nunley
Blalock, TN 37555

Dear Mrs. Nunley,

Congratulations on obtaining a grant from the Sharp Soda Foundation for supplying Blalock Middle School with new vending machines and new tables and chairs for the cafeteria.

As we know Sharp Soda and Sharp Soda Foundation have funded numerous initiatives promoting active lifestyles and educating consumers about making smart dietary choices. The key principle behind all of these efforts is balancing nutrition and physical activity. These new vending machines will provide Blalock students with more varied food and beverage choices while increasing income for the School Nutrition Program.

Again, congratulations on your excellent performance in obtaining this sizeable grant from Sharp Soda Foundation.

Sincerely,
Angela Michaels, Director
TN Nutrition Board
Administration Building
1100 Middle School Avenue
Nashville, TN 37243-0389
Phone:(555)555-5555 or 1-800-555-FOOD

Cc: Mrs. Reardon

TNutrition Board

Blalock School Lunch Administrator
Mrs. Nunley
Blalock, TN 37555

Dear Mrs. Nunley,

Congratulations on increasing income for the School Nutrition Services through the use of Sharp Soda Vending Machines.

As we know Sharp Soda and it's many food brands including Sharp Chips, Sharp Cookies, Sharp Pies and Sharp Candy are popular choices in school vending machines. Because of your diligence in choosing the more popular choices such as Sharp Candy Coated Popcorn, Sharp Corn Chips and Sharp Cookies you were able to increase income from the new vending machines by 36%.

Again, congratulations on your excellent performance in increasing income through the use of the new vending machines.

Sincerely,
Angela Michaels, Director
TN Nutrition Board
Administration Building
1100 Middle School Avenue
Nashville, TN 37243-0389
Phone:(555)555-5555 or 1-800-555-FOOD

Cc: Mrs. Reardon

I read all the papers. I saw what Becky meant. The information about the soda and vending machines were easy to understand, but the others were not.

"This is easy. Soda is not good for us, and I get that. I don't know about the things from the vending machines. Are they bad too?"

"Duh, of course they are," she said. I didn't mind her teasing me anymore. She did that with all her friends, and I knew she wasn't being mean. She was just different from the other girls I knew.

"Haven't you ever read the labels?"

"No," I confessed.

"You should. It's an education. The snacks are loaded with sugar and fat. That stuff rots your teeth and makes you fat and can cause problems with your heart and other stuff."

"How do you know?" I asked.

"Remember what my dad does? He talks to me all the time about what I should and shouldn't eat. He's an expert."

"Maybe we should meet with him again," I suggested.

"I agree. But two things we have to remember: first, he does not want to hear about our little field trip in the cafeteria, and second, I think we should have two science projects."

"Two?"

"Yes, the one we have explained to The Bear and another one that we will not tell anyone about until we set it up at the fair."

"I don't understand."

"Look," she explained, "we can't use these memos and documents because someone would ask where we got them. And my dad is serious about health and school lunches, but he would not be happy if I had to tell him where we got them. So we ask my dad about soda and vending machine junk, and he'll give us a lecture on eating right. Maybe we can ask him some questions about what the other memos say but don't tell him where we heard it. We can say we found it online, which is true. Then we will make another part of the science project that will talk about what we learned about good lunches from dad and the Internet and add it there."

"But wouldn't he ask if we were going to use the information on our project?" I asked.

"Let's hope not," she said. "I would have to tell him yes and that would make him happy, but if he ever spoke to The Bear we would have a problem. But let's not worry about that. Dad doesn't feel very welcome at school, so he doesn't speak to anyone very often."

CHAPTER TWENTY-EIGHT

The next day Becky and I were called to the office. Mr. Kohla gave us both looks like "What's this all about?" We sat outside Mrs. Reardon's office.

"If they separate us, be sure to tell them just what we told the janitor," Becky said to me.

"I will," I said. I had never been called to the principal's office, and I didn't like it. My mouth was dry, and I hoped I would be able to say anything.

The office had two desks for secretaries and a long wall with cubbies, which were used for teachers' mail. The secretary's desk belonged to Ms. Rice. She was an overweight woman with short dark hair and glasses that made her eyes look big. But she was always nice. She called everybody sweetie or honey.

"Now you two sweeties just sit there until Ms. Reardon gets done with the morning announcements. Ms. Reardon came out of her office in the back. She didn't smile very often, and when she looked at us, she didn't smile at all. She was tall and thin. She always stood up very straight and appeared to be looking down on anyone she spoke to. Her nose and eyes crowded together.

"All rise," she said.

We did.

She said the Pledge of Allegiance. "You may be seated for a moment of silence." Finally, she gave the announcements. When she finished, she went back in her office without looking at us. We sat. I watched the clock over the microphone that Ms. Reardon had just used. It was five minutes before the phone rang on Ms. Rice's desk.

"Yes, Ms. Reardon," she answered and put down the phone. She smiled at us and said, "You all can go in to Ms. Reardon's office, but be sure to knock."

We walked to the door and I knocked.

"Enter," she said.

I opened the door and let Becky go in first. Mrs. Reardon was seated at her desk, poring over some papers. She didn't look at us. There were chairs in front of her desk, but she didn't ask us to sit.

"So, what were the two of you doing sneaking around the school yesterday afternoon?" she asked without looking up.

My mouth was dry and I started to speak, but Becky beat me to it.

"We were just going back to my locker. I left some stuff here for our science project, and we needed to work on it over the weekend."

"Mr. Hurley tells me you were in the cafeteria." She still didn't look up.

"Mr. Hurley is mistaken," Becky said.

"In fact, Mrs. Nunley thinks someone was in her office." She finally looked up.

We didn't say anything.

"So what were the two of you doing in her office?"

"Who said we were in her office?" Becky replied. I was amazed at how cool she was about this. I was afraid my face was turning red.

"Oh, come on, do you expect me to believe it's just a coincidence that you two are in the building when you shouldn't be and someone breaks into Mrs. Nunley's office?"

"I can't help what you think," answered Becky. Mrs. Reardon stood up. She folded her arms across her chest and squinted her small eyes at us.

"Don't smart-mouth me. I know you're lying."

That changed everything for me. Until then I was afraid and upset because she was right about what we had done. But she couldn't really know we were there, so she was lying just like we were, although Becky hadn't actually lied about anything. Now I was angry.

"I'm just answering your questions," said Becky. She still didn't seem worried about anything.

"Is this so, RJ?" she glared at me.

"Is what so?" I asked. Not afraid now. I saw Becky's head turn to me.

"Don't be cute," she said to me. "Did you and Becky break into Mrs. Nunley's office?"

"No," I answered without hesitation. Mrs. Reardon still stared at me. In fact, we hadn't broken in. All the doors were open.

"Well, I don't believe either one of you," she snarled. "And if you ever do anything like this again, I'll suspend you from school."

Becky turned back to her. "Are you saying that we are lying?" Becky asked. Now she had an annoyed tone to her voice.

"What do you think?" asked Mrs. Reardon.

"I think my dad will be interested to hear that you just called me a liar."

"Get back to your classes," she commanded. I turned to go, but Becky still stared at Mrs. Reardon.

"Now," said the principal.

I held the door for Becky.

When we got to the hallway, Becky said, "Well, that went well." She was smiling. "By the way, you were good in there. Thanks for helping me."

"But she was right. We did it and we were lying. I don't like that. That's not what my parents taught me." I was still angry with Mrs. Reardon, but I couldn't believe that Becky didn't care about lying.

"Listen to me," she said. "First of all, I never lied. But I know that I didn't tell the whole truth and that was wrong. And I don't like it either. But Mrs. Reardon was lying too. She said we did something, even though she has no idea whether we did or not. I don't respect adults who lie to me. Adults are supposed to be adults. We're just kids. Do you think that Mr. Kohla or your mom would lie to us? And there are times when adults won't tell us the truth. Then we have to find out the truth for ourselves. That's the reason we had to be in Mrs. Nunley's office. She wouldn't tell us the truth either."

My head hurt. Most of what she said was true, but I still knew what we had done was wrong. I was very confused. This was not simple and I wished it could be. I wanted to talk to Mom and Dad about this, but I knew I couldn't.

And I had to admit that I liked Becky a lot. She was smart, pretty, and a good friend. She also liked me. I knew that now. And she didn't treat me as if I were a loser like some of the other university kids did.

CHAPTER TWENTY-NINE

THURSDAY, MAY 5
RJ AND BECKY

I was still in the hallway at my locker when Mr. Kohla stopped to talk with me.

"I need to see you and Becky as soon as she gets here," he said.

"OK, is something wrong?" I asked.

He didn't answer immediately, and he looked a little disturbed.

"I don't think so," he said and walked back to the classroom.

I saw Becky coming down the hall with her friends. I walked up to her.

"We need to talk," I said. The other girls gave me a look like "we know what's going on." They didn't have a clue, but they walked away.

"Mr. Kohla wants to see us," I said.

"I'm not surprised," she answered.

"You're not? Why don't I know what's going on?"

"Because it's about what my father did."

Oh, no, I thought. *Just what I don't want: Becky making a mess of this and then I can't do my job.*

"What'd he do?" I asked.

"When I told him that Mrs. Reardon called us liars, he went ballistic. He wanted all the details. So I told him."

"I'm guessing you didn't tell him everything."

"You would be right, just the stuff that happened in the room. He came to school right away to talk to her."

"What did he say?" I asked.

"Well, he didn't tell me everything, but reading between the lines, he told her she had no business calling us liars and that if it ever happened again, he would go to the Board of Education with a lawyer and ask for her dismissal. He obviously got her attention. I don't think she'll bother us again."

"What do you think Mr. Kohla wants?" I asked.

"Let's find out," she said and walked into the class.

We went right to Mr. Kohla's desk.

"I need to talk to you two for a minute or so after homeroom; stay around for a while and I'll write you a pass to your next class."

We said fine. When everyone left, we stayed.

"I just want to double-check on your project and didn't want to take class time. You are writing a survey for the eighth grade about their feelings about lunches. Right?"

"Yes, that's why we needed the menus," said Becky.

"OK, and then you are going to watch the kids and keep records of what they choose to eat."

"That's right," I said.

"Anything else?" he asked.

"Not now," said Becky. "I am looking on the Internet for stuff about lunches for comparisons. In fact, I was just going to tell RJ about a site I found called schoollunchbox.org. I haven't read much yet though."

"But all you need from the cafeteria is to watch the kids pick food at lunch."

"That's right," I replied.

"OK." He looked relieved. Here are your passes.

On the way to class, I asked Becky, "So what's up with school-lunchbox.org?"

"You know we can't use the stuff we found in the office now, so I found this great site about healthy lunches and it gives examples. I'm thinking we should compare good lunches to ours."

"That might work," I said. "Then it would have nothing to do with our cafeteria visit."

"Yup," she said. "And by way, I wrote the survey and I'm giving it out this week. When I get the results, I will give them to you and you should plan to do your job of watching the lunch line set up. Meanwhile, I will do some looking at schoollunchbox.org, and you should too."

We went on to our classes. So the project looked OK. I did not see any way it could be connected to Mrs. Nunley's stuff. And maybe the new website would help.

That night, I went online and checked out schoollunchbox.org. Becky was right; there was a lot of advice about how to stay healthy. It was written specifically for kids. The information would help us compare a healthy lunch to our school lunch.

SchoolLunchBox.org is a tool to help kids make healthy choices when eating school lunches.

A school lunch must provide 1/3 of the Recommended Dietary Allowances for lunch and be consistent with Dietary Guidelines for Americans.

Every lunch must include one choice from each of the following groups:

❖Meat/Alternative: A two ounce serving (edible portion) of lean meat, poultry, fish, cheese; one-half cup cottage cheese, 1 cup yogurt; one large egg; four tablespoons peanut butter; one-half cup cooked dry beans; other nut and seed butters.

❖Fruit/Vegetable: A three-fourth cup serving of two or more fruits and/or vegetables.

❖Grain: Eight servings per week of an enriched or whole-grain bread or grain product; rice; enriched pasta product.

❖Milk: One-half pint of fluid whole milk and unflavored low-fat milk must be offered.

❖Students must choose at least 3 of the choices offered. Soda or junk foods are not allowed to be available during lunch hours.

Click on the links above to learn more about making healthy choices in each group.

| Home | **_Meat/Alternative_** | Fruit/Vegetable | Grain | Milk |

Meat/Alternative: A two ounce serving (edible portion) of lean meat, poultry, fish, or cheese; one-half cup cottage cheese, 1 cup yogurt; one large egg; four tablespoons peanut butter; one-half cup cooked dry beans; other nut and seed butters.

Beans are a great choice. Whenever possible choose beans as a meat alternative.

Eat This	Not This
Baked chicken nuggets	Fried chicken nuggets
Baked spicy chicken on a bun	Cheeseburger
Spaghetti with marina sauce	Spaghetti with meat sauce
Bean and cheese burrito	Steak and Cheese Sub
Turkey sandwich	Corn dog
Baked fish sandwich	Ham Hoagie
Chili	Cheese sticks

School LunchBox.Org

Home Meat/Alternative *Fruit/Vegetable* Grain Milk

Eat This
Fresh fruit
Green Beans
Broccoli
Strawberries
Apple
Salad

Not This
Fruit juice
Cheesy green beans
Cheese broccoli
Strawberry pie
Apple sauce
Onion rings

Fruit/Vegetable: A three-fourth cup serving of two or more fruits and/or vegetables.

Fruit:

The best choices of fruit are any that are fresh, frozen or canned without added sugars.

Choose canned fruits in juice or light syrup

Dried fruit and fruit juice are also nutritious choices, but the portion sizes are small so they may not be as filling as other choices.

Vegetables:

Starchy vegetables like potatoes, corn, and peas are included in the "Whole Grain Foods" section because they contain more carbohydrate.

Fresh vegetables are best choices because they have less sodium than canned or frozen vegetables.

School LunchBox.Org

Home Meat/Alternative Fruit/Vegetable *Grain* Milk

Eat This
Whole wheat bread
Oatmeal bread/crackers
Whole wheat pasta
Brown rice
Whole wheat tortilla
Corn/peas

Not This
Whole wheat cookies
Oatmeal cookies
White pasta
White rice
Enriched tortilla
corn bread

Grain: Eight servings per week of an enriched or whole-grain bread or grain product; rice; enriched pasta product.

The most popular grain in the US is wheat. To make 100% whole wheat flour, the entire wheat grain is ground up. "Refined" flours like white and enriched wheat flour include only part of the grain – the starchy part, and are not whole grain. They are missing many of the nutrients found in whole wheat flour. Examples of whole grain wheat products include 100% whole wheat bread, pasta, tortilla, and crackers.

Popcorn is also a whole grain but be sure not to add lots of butter or salt.

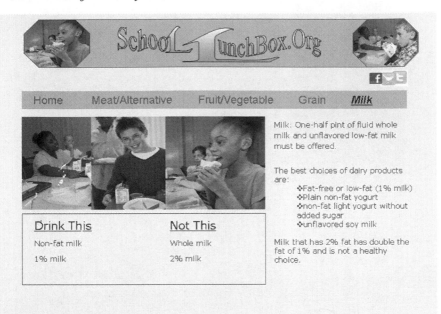

School LunchBox.Org

Home   Meat/Alternative   Fruit/Vegetable   Grain   *Milk*

Drink This	Not This
Non-fat milk	Whole milk
1% milk	2% milk

Milk: One-half pint of fluid whole milk and unflavored low-fat milk must be offered.

The best choices of dairy products are:
- Fat-free or low-fat (1% milk)
- Plain non-fat yogurt
- non-fat light yogurt without added sugar
- unflavored soy milk

Milk that has 2% fat has double the fat of 1% and is not a healthy choice.

CHAPTER THIRTY

SATURDAY, APRIL 23
LAMAR

One of the things I like about my computer: the games. Of course most of them are silly and way too easy, but *The Galaxy of Death* is awesome. Unfortunately I don't have the money to buy it, but when I was talking about it to my friend Dwayne at school, he told me about a two-week free trial that I could sign up for. I was ecstatic. I couldn't wait to get home and sign up.

After signing up, I created my avatar and named myself the Lamarinator. It was way cool. The Lamarinator was one of the good guys, like my friend Dwayne. Our goal was to eliminate all the evil ones who were trying to take over the galaxy and enslave the rest of us. I made mistakes, but I learned quickly. Dwayne gave me a huge magazine all about how to play the game. I read it in one night. Dwayne and I formed an alliance with four other heroes. We arranged the times we would log on, and then we worked together as I team. We called ourselves the Galactilytes. We were able to communicate through chats. In the chat area, we spoke to each other, but only members of the team could hear. There was a bark command, which we used if we needed to warn someone.

After a week of playing, I was getting a little bored hanging out with the other Galactilytes. The game has forty levels, and I wanted to move through them and see how far I could go alone. I had read in the game's magazine that if a player moves too quickly through the levels, the game shuts down and a "kill screen" appears, which terminates your play. Apparently only superstar players have ever experienced that. I wanted to see how fast I could move without the kill screen appearing and see if I could post the fastest time to level forty. Mama and Jeane both work on Saturdays, so I waited until they were gone to start. I tried to pace myself the way some of the super players wrote about in the magazine. The superstars' times were posted at each level. So I used my watch to help me move just a little faster through each level.

I concentrated and started moving up quickly. By the time I was at thirty-five, I was a full two minutes ahead of the fastest time. I was sweating, but I could not stop. Finally I reached level forty, and I was sure I could beat the best time. One more move and…

My screen went blank. Then there was a little flash and a series of numbers, letters, and figures started rolling across the screen. They didn't make any sense to me. I highlighted all the data, and when it stopped scrolling, I copied it into a document file. Then nothing happened, and I couldn't get the computer to do anything, so I shut it down and went to have some lunch.

CHAPTER THIRTY-ONE

SATURDAY, APRIL 23
LAMAR

My cellphone rang right after I finished eating. I answered it.

"Turn the computer back on now. Do it now or the police will be at your door in fifteen minutes." The voice was flat, almost mechanical. Then the caller was gone.

I looked at the clock. Fifteen minutes? What should I do? What had I done? I went to the computer and turned it on.

When I got online, there was a blinking icon in the left corner. It was my name. I had never seen anything like it before. I clicked on the icon, and the screen went dark. Only the cursor was visible. Suddenly, the cursor moved, and words started to appear on the screen.

It read: "Lamar, you have entered a secure section of *The Galaxy of Death*. How did you do this?" The words stopped and were followed by "Galactolocator911."

"I don't know," I typed.

"I don't believe you. Convince me." Galactolocator911.

I typed as fast as I could.

"I was just playing the game."

"No one plays the game that well."

"But that's all I was doing. I was trying to beat the fastest score."

There was nothing for a minute or so. I wasn't sure if that was good or bad. I could feel my heart racing and sweat was pouring off my forehead.

Finally. "You copied a set programming at the end of the game. Why?" Galactolocater911.

"I don't know. I was just curious."

"That data contains information that is classified by the federal government. Do you understand?" Galactolocator911.

"No. I mean yes, but I didn't know that."

Silence again.

"First, you must erase the file you saved in your documents. I have access to your computer. If you do not do this, I will know. Second, you must never play the game again. Our *conversation* here is encrypted and will be permanently deleted at the end. Clear?" Galactolocator911.

"Yes," I wrote back.

"If you don't follow my instructions, federals agents will visit you. Do you understand?" Galactolator911.

"Yes, I understand." But I really didn't.

That was all. My screen returned to my home page.

CHAPTER THIRTY-TWO

SATURDAY, APRIL 23
LAMAR

What had I done? I'm only a kid. How could that guy control my computer and know what was on it? How did he get my cell phone number? I'd seen stuff like that on TV, but I wasn't convinced it could happen in real life. But obviously it could.

I decided to watch TV. I didn't want to ever look at the computer again.

Both Mama and Jeane were out; Mama works at the thrift shop, and Jeane helps in the library.

My cell phone rang. I jumped.

"Hello," I answered.

"Turn your computer on," said a voice I recognized. Then he hung up. I was numb. Should I do what he said? Should I tell Jeane what was going on? Or Mama?

I went into my room and turned it on. The icon with my name was flashing again. I clicked it.

The screen went dark again.

"Lamar, you know who this is. We need to talk. Can you use Skype?" Galactolocator911.

"Yes," I typed.

NO Book One of 8th Day Series

"Good, open up Skype. If there is someone at home with you, turn the volume down."

The screen blinked, and I was back to the Internet. I opened Skype. Almost immediately it started ringing. I accepted the call.

I could see my picture in a small box at the bottom of the screen. Behind it was a larger screen where I could see a room. The room was a mess. Clothes were all over the floor. I could see a pizza box on a table. It was open. Below it were napkins, dirty napkins on the floor. Cans of soda were on the table and the floor. I could see some posters on the wall of rock groups. I recognized Metallica, Black Sabbath, and Whitesnake. The room was small, and a bright light from the side made everything in the room stand out, but I saw no one.

"Don't look for me," a voice said—the same voice from the telephone.

"No, sir," I said. He must have been standing to the side of the computer because I couldn't see him.

"Don't call me, sir," the voice laughed.

"What should I call you?"

"For now, the guardian will do."

"What do you want from me?" I asked.

"Oh, I've got a bunch of questions, and you better answer them," he replied. The voice didn't sound old or young, but somewhere in between.

"All right," I said.

"First, is there anyone home?"

"No. My Mama and sister both work on Saturdays."

"Good. Let's start with the game, Lamar."

"How do you know my name?" I asked. Then I was afraid I'd make him angry.

128

"I know all about you and your family," the voice answered with a little laugh again. "But don't worry. I come in peace...maybe." He thought that was really funny. I didn't.

"What do you want to know about the game?" I asked.

"I know you are a techno hot shot, little kid, but I still have a hard time believing you could beat the game so fast."

"Well, it's true. I've been working on it for a while. I read magazines about it and talked to people. Computers and stuff come easy to me."

"I can relate to that. And by the way, in case you are thinking of recording or saving this Skype session, forget about it. I don't doubt you think you are, and maybe you are bright enough to do it, but I'm better. This session has an internal virus, and when we are done it will wipe both computers clean of our conversation. You got that?"

"Yes."

"But do you know what you did?"

"No," I said. I think my voice was getting a little shaky.

"Kids are always looking for secret levels and backdoors. Most never get anywhere. Somehow you got to the source code and reached the abstraction level. You were in a place that has proprietary information. Really good hackers can do that, and then if they get through the encryption, they can get the names and credit card numbers of our clients as well as other things they shouldn't have."

"But I didn't know." Now I was close to tears. "I'm sorry. I won't do it again."

"You bet you won't," he said. "I'll see to that." And then he laughed again. Was this guy crazy?

"Do you know what information was in the part of the program you breached?"

"No, I don't even know how I got there. I was just playing and when I won, I put my hands on the keyboard just to like celebrate and that screen appeared."

"So, you're telling me this was an accident."

"Yes, yes, sir."

"What did I tell you?"

"Sorry, I forgot. No more sirs."

"Well," he started. His voice was closer to, I don't know, normal now. "All that information you saw was code. But you would know that. It includes all the credit card numbers I mentioned, and it's worth a fortune to some people."

"I never knew. I'm sorry. I destroyed the codes."

"I believe you," he said. "Know why I do?"

"No," I stammered.

"Lamar Dixon, seventh grade student at Roosevelt Middle School. All A's on your report card. Jeane Dixon, sister. Senior at George Washington High School. Good student. Not as good as you. Interested in medicine. Mother, Annette Dixon. Widow of Robert Dixon. Killed in an automobile accident. Sorry about that, Lamar.

Now my voice was shaking. I wasn't sure if I was angry or scared. "How do you know that? Have you been spying on us? That's against the law. If you do anything to my family…" He interrupted.

"Cool down kid. If I wanted to do anything, I would have done it by now. And listen to me, little mister computer whiz. All that stuff is on the net. You just need to know how to find it, and I do. Don't you know the government and other people know just about everything there is to know about you? It's all out there in cyberspace. You of all people should know that."

I had read stuff about what he was saying, but I wasn't sure it was true.

We were both quiet for a while.

"So, why are you so interested in me?" I asked.

"I see a kindred spirit in you," he said.

"A what?"

"I mean we're a lot alike."

"How are we alike?" I asked.

"Obviously we both like computers and technology. And it's clear we both like to push the edges; you know, do what others can't or won't. But most of all, we both risk getting into trouble. Actually I saved you from a world of bad news."

"I wasn't going to use those credit cards."

"I know that, but there was a lot more there."

"Like what?"

He was quiet.

"Don't stop now," I said.

"Yeah, well it's complicated," he said. " But I think you're worth the risk. You're good enough with computers that you are likely to get in trouble again, and maybe then you won't meet someone as forgiving as me."

"So," I persisted.

"So...the data you saw also has highly classified government information and listening posts."

"What are you talking about?"

"You know those rooms you go into to talk with your friends about the game?" he asked.

"Sure. They're private so no one can hear what we talk about."

"You wish," he said. "There are people like me who listen all the time."

"Why would people listen to junk about the game that me and my friends talk about?" I asked.

"They're not interested in you. They're interested in some serious bad guys. Guys who blow up things. Guys who try to steal government secrets about weapons systems and other things that go boom."

"I don't get it," I said.

"Most people don't," he said. He sounded serious now. "There's a lot you don't know, but listen and learn, my little geek."

CHAPTER THIRTY-THREE

SATURDAY, APRIL 23
LAMAR

I heard the Guardian sigh.

"After 9/11, the country started taking terrorists seriously. And part of that was trying to find out what was being planned, not waiting until something bad happened."

"Yeah, I have heard about that. Airport security and junk," I said.

"That's important, but that's part of what everybody knows. Have you heard of the Patriot Act?" he asked.

"Sure. It's a way the government helps take care of us," I said.

"Yup, that's the idea. But sometimes it doesn't work the way you think."

"What do you mean by that?"

"We'll get to that later. Anyway, one of parts of staying ahead of the bad guys, and I'm all for that, is getting to know what they are thinking about. That's where I come in. I am a listening post. Whenever people are playing *The Galaxy of Death* and they go into those private rooms to talk, I listen. Almost everything I hear is just junk, but we know some dangerous people pretend to be gamers and meet in these rooms. Then they talk about what they would like to do to harm Americans. Some are stupid enough to just talk straight out about their ideas and plans. Then I report them, and Homeland Security goes into action. But some of these guys are smart enough to use a kind of code language that sounds like gamer talk but isn't. It takes someone like me to know the difference. I listen for certain words or mistakes they make in their pretending to be gamers and then it's off to the Feds."

"Well that sounds cool," I said. "You are doing something important. But I still don't get how that connects to me."

"It does and it doesn't. You were in an area where records of credit cards are stored. I had to be sure you weren't going to use that info. But the bad guys also hide things like financial records back there too, and it's a way to catch them. I knew quickly you weren't one of them, but you still had to get out."

"And I did. So why call me?" I asked.

"Because, as I said before, you and me are a lot alike."

"We are. How?" I asked.

"Let me tell you a story," he said.

CHAPTER THIRTY-FOUR

SATURDAY, APRIL 23
LAMAR

"When I was in college, I had a scholarship to study advanced technology. I got the scholarship because I was really good at the stuff, but also because I didn't have much money. My parents weren't around and that's another story, but I was living in an apartment above a garage owned by my aunt and uncle. Everything was good for the first three years. I was knocking them dead at school. I spent all my time studying. Sound like anyone you know?" he asked.

"Yeah, me," I said.

"Bingo. But in my senior year I met a girl, and well, she actually liked me and she understood most of what I was working on. I never had time for girls before, or the money. Not that she cared about the money, but I wanted to…well…take her out on a real date. Buy her dinner and a movie. You know, or you will. I couldn't ask my uncle for the money. I wasn't even paying them rent. So I stepped over the line. I hacked into a few bank accounts of some local people and got their ATM numbers. That, with a dummy card I bought from another guy who is a computer freak and totally antigovernment, allowed me to withdraw twenty dollars from five accounts. I was hoping that it was so little they wouldn't notice, and they didn't, but Big Brother noticed."

"Big Brother?" I asked.

"It's in a book you should read, but anyway it was your not-so-friendly neighborhood federal agency. You won't believe it. They arrived at my apartment, broke down my door, and came in with assault weapons raised. They can do that you know. They convinced some judge that I might be the head of some terrorist cell. Turns out it was just little old me, and were they pissed. They dragged me down to the police station and grilled me. When they finally believed me, they were still angry that I had wasted their time, but who knew?"

"So, did they arrest you?" I asked.

"Not exactly. They told me I had committed at least four felonies and if they wanted to they could put me in prison for a number of years. I almost wet my pants. *But,* they said there was a better way. They had checked up on me and knew what I could do, so they offered to drop the charges under the condition that I work for them. So here I am doing good things. And it is good, but what choice did I have. What kind of computer work would a guy with prison time for a felony get? You guessed it. Nada, zip. So I volunteered to help my country. I started right away. They set me up in my apartment, and I graduated last year. I'm waiting for them to tell me how long I have to do this, but I'm not asking right now."

"What did your aunt and uncle say?"

"Well they weren't home when it happened, and no one can see my door, which is in the back. So they only saw the broken door. But the cops came over anyway and explained they had made a mistake and had the door fixed. They also set me up with primo gear, so I can get just about anything I want from my set up. They

136

are watching me I know, but I have set up an alarm system that tells me when they are in my kitchen, so they think I'm a good little spy. Which I kinda am."

I wasn't worried about this guy anymore, and I actually liked him. But why was he telling me all of this?

"Because, like I said, I checked up on you and we are two of a kind, and I wanted to warn you to be careful. Always assume someone is watching or listening."

That worried me. How was I supposed to help the 8th Day gang if I was being watched? So I thought I'd take a chance.

"Listen to me, Guardian. I am very glad we met. And I am glad you wanted to help me because I need help."

"I don't think I'm going to like this," he said.

"No, it's not really illegal. No money is involved. But I am part of something I can't tell you about, and I might need some help at some point. You don't have to do anything if you're afraid of being caught."

"No problem there," he said. "Now that I'm part of the establishment, I am safe. They think they've got me all tucked away. But they're not the watcher. I am. Still, I don't want you in trouble. That was the point of this."

"I have no plans of getting into trouble. I've always got a back door if I need it. Besides, this stuff is really important and will be helping a lot of kids. But that's all I can tell you. So are you in?"

He never hesitated. "I'm in. And by the way, if you need to contact me, just use Skype. Look at your screen and you will see a number. Use that number."

CHAPTER THIRTY-FIVE

Spring break and a week of school had passed, and I hadn't heard anything from this group I joined. In fact I hadn't seen Uncle Jerry, which was unusual. Maybe 8th Day was just a joke. I wouldn't put it past my uncle. When I'm on break, he normally spends mucho time with me because he knows my mom and dad are going to be working big time, which is mostly what they do all the time. But no Uncle Jerry. It was Carmella and I. Instead of just cleaning the house, she stays with me on vacations. We don't talk much because her English is not great, but it's better than my Spanish. Mine is *muy poquito*, which I think means very little or something like that. But she keeps me fed, and I have to tell her where I'm going if I leave the house, which wasn't often because most of my so-called friends were off on vacations with their families. Mom told me she was in the middle of some big-time junk, and Dad was booked making old people think they looked young again.

"I'm really sorry, Karstan. I know we talked about going to the islands, but one of my firm's accounts has some things that need to be done now, and Dad just scheduled a bunch of operations, which will make us a lot of money," she told me.

Us? I thought.

I kept texting my friends while she talked. She hates that. And even more than the texting, she hates it when I say, "whatever."

So I said, "whatever." I expected a lecture, which I was prepared to ignore, but she was quiet. Maybe she did feel bad.

Oh, well, whatever.

So it was like a mildly big surprise when Uncle Jerry showed up on Saturday. I was doing my usual: texting my friends and playing *The Galaxy of Death* when he walked in.

"Another wasted day in the life of Karstan Petersen."

I rolled my eyes. "Whatever," I said.

"What a vocabulary," he replied.

"Whatever," I repeated.

He laughed.

"Well," he said, "that stops today."

That got my attention, and I looked up. Uncle Jerry was in his usual attire: sandals, jeans, and a tie-dyed shirt. I don't get how old people think that's better than low riders and spiked bracelets.

"Yup," he said as he sat down. "Today, K-man, you start work as a spy."

"Gimme a break," I said. "Is this about that guy hiding in the dark and those other lame kids? Because I have seen and heard *nada*. I figure this is just your way of getting me to be weird like you."

He was quiet, pretty unusual for him, and he didn't laugh.

"No BS, Karstan. The time's up." He sounded serious, and that never happens. And he called me by my real name, which he hates.

"We need you to do something for us. It's not going to be easy, and remember you can quit any time. This involves getting into your mom's computer and finding some files we need to have—if they are there. We don't even know that. But I know this means doing something your parents can't know about and wouldn't like if they did. So if you can't do it, I respect that." He paused like I was supposed to think.

"I mean it," he continued, "if this makes you uncomfortable..." He stopped.

"Yeah, that's likely," I said. And I think both of us were surprised.

CHAPTER THIRTY-SIX

SATURDAY, APRIL 23
KARSTAN

"OK," said Uncle Jerry. "Here's the deal. Your mom's firm has a client. This client is enormous, and their main area of work is food—food of all kinds that winds up on our tables, or as feed for farm animals, and even in school lunches. It's called AgraInc. One of its subsidiaries, which means a smaller part of the bigger company..."

"I know what it means. Don't treat me like I'm lame," I said.

"No offense. Anyway this subsidiary, SchoolMeals, deals with the food that winds up in the school lunch program. 8th Day is confident the stuff they feed you at school is not only unhealthy..."

"And doesn't taste very good," I said, "except for the pizza."

"Well, pizza is part of the problem, but what I was saying was that there are many people who know more than I do who believe the food is actually hurting the kids. As I told you before, the major concern is obesity, but also all the illnesses associated with obesity."

"Like diabetes," I said.

"So you were listening?"

"Don't tell anybody," I said. "It would ruin my reputation."

"I promise," he laughed. "So, now comes the hard part. 8th Day needs information they can use to make the public aware of the health problems threatening kids. You are a key to that. I am sure your mom has a computer here in the house."

"Of course."

"And I'm sure she uses it mostly for work."

"Right again. I don't think she's a secret gamer."

"There is a good possibility she has records, reports, or memos somewhere on her computer that could help us. We just need to get a hold of them and make them public."

Now I was interested, but I had questions.

"Let me get this straight. You want me to get on Mom's computer and steal work stuff that 8th Day can use."

"Steal is such a strong word. If you borrow it but still leave it there, is it stealing?" he asked.

"Yeah, I would think so. But I could do it. It's not like I care about those companies. But I have two questions. First, why don't you do it yourself?"

"Well, I don't know much about computers," he admitted.

"That's for sure," I said.

"And if something went wrong, I would be one of the first people the authorities would look at. And although I don't care about that, I don't want to screw up the work of 8th Day. Remember, that's one of the reasons you were chosen to help. Who's going to look at a seventh grader for stealing…uh…borrowing computer files?"

"OK, I get that, but my second question is what do I do if I need help with the computer stuff? I'm not much of a geek, and you're no help."

"Sad but true," he said.

I had a thought.

"Wait a minute. I know the answer. When we got together with Dr. A...."

"Don't tell me anything more," he said. "It's better if I don't know, and I don't want to know."

"All right, Uncle Jerry, I have my assignment, and I know you will be disavowing any knowledge of this if I get caught."

"You watch too many movies, and this mission is not impossible. I hope."

"Forget *Mission Impossible;* I'm now the *Man From Uncle.*"

CHAPTER THIRTY-SEVEN

I was psyched. This was like being in my own computer game. I thought about dressing in camouflage and blackening my face. Then I remembered it was my own house, and actually getting at Mom's computer wouldn't be hard. I was the only one in the house most of the time. Except for Carmella. I would have to look out for her. I was getting stoked. I started to call Brian who passes for my best friend, but I stopped. This really wasn't a game. It might be fun and a little dangerous, but it was the real world not a computer image, and I was no avatar.

Mom was home for dinner, which was somewhat of an occasion, and she was doing the cooking. This meant putting some packaged ravioli in boiling water and warming some Italian bread, but I always liked it better when she cooked and didn't just bring stuff home from God knows where. Dad made it too. So we ate together. Of course Mom's phone went off twice, and she had to get up and talk so it was hard to have a conversation. That made me angry, but I didn't say anything. I never do. What's the point? I mean I love her and Dad, but I seem like an afterthought. And then when they're ready to talk, which is rare, they get pissed when I don't want to. You would think they would figure it out. No way.

After dinner, I heard Mom go up to the office, so I thought I would reconnoiter the place. When I pushed open the door, she was at the computer and I startled her. She was still dressed in her business suit.

"Sorry," I said, but I wasn't.

She had glasses on, which she only used for reading. My friends tell me she is beautiful, and I guess she is. She has blonde hair cut short and very light skin with blue eyes, which she says she got from the German side of her family. Dad, on the other hand, might have been a hunk once, but he's almost fat now. His red hair is disappearing quickly. I saw a picture of him playing basketball in high school. He's more than six feet tall, and in the picture he is skinny and has long hair. I wonder sometimes what happened to that guy.

"No, no," she said. "You just surprised me. You never come up here."

"I did now."

"Yes, you did," she said. "Is there something I can do for you?"

"No, I just wanted to tell you I was glad you cooked dinner."

"Thanks." She smiled. "I know I don't do it often enough."

"It's OK," I said. "I like your computer."

"Did you want one like it? I..."

No," I said. "I was just looking at it."

"Well, sit down and try it. I was just logging on."

"No, that's OK," I said.

"I insist. You can get it started for me."

I sat down. It was an IBM and it was a monster. I don't know how good it would be with games, but this was a serious piece of machinery. I turned it on and a page opened asking for a user ID and password.

"OK," Mom said. "Type in blueeyeddevil. That's me."

I didn't want to ask.

"Now type in porshe356b. That's a car I used to own."

I pressed return and the screen was up. Her default page was her law firm. No big surprise there.

"Do you want to see it do anything in particular?"

"Sure," I said. "Let's see how fast it is."

I went to Facebook and logged in. It was hyper speed. There was stuff there from all my friends that I didn't want her to see, so I logged right out.

"That's cool," I said and got up.

"Oh, you don't have to leave," she said.

"It's OK. I know you have work to do." I think she looked relieved.

CHAPTER THIRTY-EIGHT

SUNDAY, APRIL 30
GRACIELA

I followed Miss Fuentes suggestions all week. I didn't have another problem with my eyes, but I still worried. I was very young, but I remembered my mother and some of the things she had to do because of her diabetes. I didn't want to have diabetes.

On Sunday I met Miss Fuentes at the Center. We went to her office.

"OK, let me show you the site," she said. She opened her computer and there it was. It was bright and colorful and showed pictures of kids my age in school, playing outside, and just having fun. The site highlighted tips on staying healthy through exercise and proper nutrition. And it was fun!

"Wow," I said. "This is wonderful."

Welcome

BFIT is for kids – kids helping kids stay healthy. We're the first generation of kids that are getting diseases that only old people use to get. Why? It's called obesity.

Here are the facts:

> ➢Obesity means an excess of body fat – over 25% in boys or over 32% in girls.

> ➢Obesity has more than tripled in the last 20 years and one in every three kids is either overweight or obese.

> ➢Obesity increases our chances of getting asthma, diabetes, high blood pressure, high cholesterol, heart disease, liver problems, bone problems, breathing problems such as sleep apnea, rashes and infections of the skin.

> ➢Adults haven't been able to help so we need to help ourselves. We can do it together.

Sign up and join us -- become part of "Our Gang"!

BFIT Team

Staying Healthy

What do we have to do to stay healthy?

Here are the facts:

> ➢We have to eat more healthy foods and less junk foods.

> ➢We have to exercise at least 60 minutes every day.

> ➢We have to get at least 8 hours of sleep every night.

> ➢We have to play fewer video games and play games that help us keep moving.

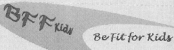

Eating Healthy

What do we have to do to eat healthy?

Here are the facts:

>Use the MyPlate picture to help you when you fill your plate for each meal.

>Fill your plate at any given meal with more vegetables, fruits, and whole grains, which naturally have more nutrients.

>Skip add-ons like batters, breading, and butter, and choose sauces and dressings wisely, like vinaigrettes made with healthy olive oil instead of full-fat dressings.

>Opt for a baked potato instead of French fries, grilled chicken instead of fried, brown rice instead of white rice, and non-fat milk instead of whole milk or soda.

>Eat fewer solid fats like high fat meats, butter, lard, cream and eat fewer foods with lots of sugar. Eat fruits and veggies for snacks.

>Eat more fish.

See *Recipes* for easy ways to eat healthy.

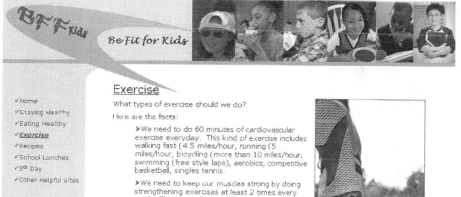

Exercise

What types of exercise should we do?

Here are the facts:

>We need to do 60 minutes of cardiovascular exercise everyday. This kind of exercise includes walking fast (4.5 miles/hour, running (5 miles/hour, bicycling (more than 10 miles/hour, swimming (free style laps), aerobics, competitive basketball, singles tennis.

>We need to keep our muscles strong by doing strengthening exercises at least 2 times every week. This can include such things as playing on playground equipment, climbing trees, and playing tug-of-war, or structured activities such as lifting weights or working with resistance bands.

>We need to do bone strengthening exercises at least 3 times every week. This type of exercise produces a force on the bones that promotes bone growth and strength. This force is commonly produced by impact with the ground. Running, jumping rope, basketball, tennis, and hopscotch are all examples of bone strengthening activities. As these examples illustrate, bone-strengthening activities can also be aerobic and muscle-strengthening.

"And now, it's all yours," she said. "I have made you the host. I didn't use your real name or where you are from, of course. But it is you. And now you will be hosting it. You can work out of this office. Every few days I will update the site with new recipes or health hints. There is a chat section; you can chat with the users and answer questions if you know the answers. If you don't, tell them you will get back to them. Then you can ask me, and I will find the answers."

"It sounds like you are doing all the work," I said.

"For now," she answered, "but your time comes soon. You can see this site is designed for kids ten through fifteen, and I need you to be the one talking to them. They would know I was an adult right away. Remember when you chat, never tell anything about yourself. That brings me to another item. There is a place here, (she pointed to the screen) where kids are asked to sign in and get regular posts about good health. To sign up they need only give their age, e-mail address, and what school they attend. Nothing else. Everyone is protected. So when you chat, remind users to keep out private personal things that could identify them. I know this is a lot of work, and if it's too much say so."

"No I want to do it. If it's OK, I will tell my aunt that I will come to the center in the evenings where you will help me with school-work. She likes you a lot. And I can always use help with my home-work."

"I doubt that, but it sounds like a good plan."

CHAPTER THIRTY-NINE

THURSDAY, MAY 5
RJ AND BECKY

Becky had taken the menus and e-mails home and copied them so I could have my own set. After speaking to Ryan, I knew what I had to do. I had received an e-mail from Lamar the week before. It had my phony Facebook name and password. His e-mail simply said: Browne, redflower, and Luke. When I got it, I copied down the information and immediately trashed the e-mail. I tried out the name and password and they worked perfectly. I had my own wall and a picture of a red flower. I knew Lamar was Luke but nothing else. I did a test drive. I sent Lamar a message asking, "How's the weather? How often do you check?" The next day I logged in to my new shadow account and there was a message from Luke. It simply said, "Weather is cool. Check every afternoon."

I went back to the things we had gotten from Mrs. Nunley's office and to the menus she had given us. There were three memos from people in our school district and from people in Nashville. Becky had told me she would not show the memos to her dad because he would want to know where they had come from. She and her dad planned to go over the menus and see how, and if, they were serving what they should be as well as how healthy the menus were.

Becky wrote a survey for the eighth graders asking them what they liked and disliked about the school lunches and what they ate. After collecting the surveys we would sit in the cafeteria and check what choices the kids were really making and compare that information to the surveys. It would make for a good poster to use in the science fair.

But first I would have to get the information to Lamar. I waited until Thursday because mom is always late on Thursdays, and then she goes right to work at the restaurant.

I hurried home from school, logged in to Facebook, and wrote to Luke.

"Hey, Luke. Are you there?"

"Yes, Sam."

"I have several things for you. How do I get them there?" I asked.

"Can you scan things?" he asked.

"Yes, there is a scanner with the printer."

"Good," he replied. "Scan and e-mail what you have along with any notes to this address."

He gave me an e-mail address. I wrote it down and put it in my pocket.

"What is this?" I asked.

"A friend's smartphone. When you send it, mention me and I will get it."

"Will do. It should be there tonight. But there is more."

"Can you send it?" he asked.

"Couldn't get it," I said. "It was protected, and I didn't know what to do."

"But you got on?"

"Yes."

"And you saw something good?"

"I think so."

"OK," said Lamar. "I'll figure out what to do."

"What are you doing, honey?" It was my mom's voice and she was right behind me. I switched the computer to a page about the Civil War I had opened before."

"Just looking at some Civil War stuff. We are going to start studying that in Ms. Perkin's class soon. What are you doing home so early?"

"Oh, I just finished up and Coach Meeks told me to go home. He knows I have to go to work tonight."

She sounded tired. When she turned around to leave my room, I closed the Facebook tab.

"I'm going to lie down for a minute. If I fall asleep, please wake me so I'm not late. Can't afford to lose that job."

"OK, Mom." The lying was getting easier, and it didn't feel good.

CHAPTER FORTY

THURSDAY, MAY 5
LAMAR

I thought that RJ had ended our talk pretty fast, and I was tempted to try to get him back online, but decided maybe he needed to be gone. He could tell me later. Rashon was supposed to come over tonight to help Jeane with her homework, and I could get the information from RJ off his smartphone. But what was more important to me was what RJ said he couldn't get. It must have been important; otherwise, he wouldn't have mentioned it. There must have been something on a computer he couldn't access, and he needed help. But so did I. I know I'm good, but getting on a computer hundreds of miles away was not something I had done.

It was time to talk to the Guardian and see if he was really up for helping us. I hadn't told him much, and if I was in his place, I would be very careful. He needed to be able to say that he didn't know what was going on, and I wasn't about to put him in danger. His apartment was awful, but it was better than a jail cell. I decided to wait until Friday night when Mom went to church and Jeane and Rashon went to the movies.

The pair walked in the door a few minutes later, and I came out of my room as they unloaded a pile of books.

"Hey guys," I said.

"Hi, Lamar," said Jeane. She was always extra nice to me when Rashon was around. That's OK.

"Rashon, have you checked your phone recently?" I asked.

"Why?"

"I am hoping you've received some items for me."

"Is this 8th stuff?" asked Jeane.

"Yes."

"Are you being careful?" she asked.

"Absolutely," I answered. *Except for the stuff about the Guardian*, I thought to myself.

Rashon looked at his phone. "Oh, yeah. There's quite a bit here. Why didn't you just have it sent to your computer?"

I looked at him without saying anything.

After a minute he said, "Right, you're being careful."

"That is what you told me isn't it?"

"You got that right. Good for you. I'm proud of you. Let's go download it to your computer," he said.

"Actually," I said, "let's just print it from your phone to my printer, and then you can erase it."

"Good thinking. I knew there was a reason I asked you to help."

We printed out RJ's documents and then the three of us looked over what he sent and tried to decide what to do with it.

"Well, it's no smoking gun," Rashon said. "But it's good stuff. I think we should push this up the line and see what the big dogs say."

"Makes sense," I said. "I'll take care of it."

"How?" asked Rashon.

"You remember what we said about not sharing too much so no one knew more than they need?" I reminded him.

"Damn," he said. "You are smart."

"Rashon," Jeane said, raising her voice.

"Sorry, dear."

They went back to the living room, and I went to work. I was the only one I knew of that had a Facebook entry for Dr. A. I used it and left a message to contact me.

Then I waited.

CHAPTER FORTY-ONE

THURSDAY, MAY 5
LAMAR

While Rashon and Jeane worked on homework in the kitchen, I went to my room and played games. I had Facebook on another screen so I could see when Dr. A came on. About fifteen minutes later, I got an e-mail asking me to chat with J. Beard, which was Dr. A's Facebook name. I switched screens.

"Luke, what do you want?" Luke Walker was the name I used. My profile listed me as a Star Wars fan.

"I have the letters you were waiting for," I said.

"Good," he answered. "I can't wait to see them. I haven't heard from cousin Sam for a long time." That was RJ's name. " How soon can I see them?"

"Right away," I said.

"Good, send them right along. And Luke, you know how personal these letters are, being about our great aunt and all. Please be sure to delete them from your files right away. I'd be embarrassed if anyone saw them."

"Of course," I said. "They should be there in a few minutes."

"Thanks, Luke, I appreciate it. I wish I could speak to Sam myself, but you know how the family is."

"I do indeed."

"Is that all?" he asked.

"Well, not exactly. Sam has some more family things, but he can't get his hands on them right away," I wrote.

"Can you help him?" J. asked.

"I think so, but I will need some time, and maybe help," I said.

"Anything I can do?" he asked.

"No, but I have it covered."

"Good," he said. "Remember, family things are private. If you need help, there is always your uncle" (that was Rashon).

"I know. Don't worry," I told him.

"I'm sure you will do the right thing," he replied. "Be safe and say hello to everyone for me."

"I will," I said. But he was gone.

I knew I needed help to get whatever it was that RJ had. He said it was protected, so that had to mean it was on a computer he couldn't get to. I knew my only hope was the Guardian. I was sure Dr. A. would want me to talk to Rashon, but Rashon doesn't know enough about computers. And besides, the less he knew, the better. This was all supposed to be about everybody knowing as little as possible. If someone questioned Rashon, he couldn't tell the person what he didn't know.

But the Guardian was going to take some work. I knew he said he was in, but that was before I asked for anything. I had to give it a try. If it didn't work, then I would talk to Rashon.

CHAPTER FORTY-TWO

FRIDAY, MAY 6
LAMAR

It was Friday night. I waited till Mama, Jeane, and Rashon were all gone. Mama asked if I wanted to come along, but I said I had too much homework. A little bit of a stretch. I punched up a game screen so I could go back to it if anyone walked in on me. Then I went to Skype. The Guardian had given me a name and number to reach him. He said if he didn't answer, he would be able to see I had called and he would call back. I needed to catch a break. I needed him now.

I put the call in. I must have been living right, because he answered immediately. The screen came on. I could see his room. Hard to miss the mess. I turned on the microphone.

"What's up, geek boy?" he said.

I still couldn't see him.

"You remember that stuff I was talking to you about?"

"You mean that spy junk, that secret agent stuff," he laughed.

"You don't know how close you are," I said. That got his attention.

"Now wait a minute, 007. Are you in trouble? Are you going to be in trouble?"

"I certainly hope not," I said. "I'm cool, but I need your help."

"OK, tell me about it." He wasn't laughing now.

"I've got a friend who has access to a computer, which has some files on it he can't open. And we need to see those files."

"Tell me this is not a government agency or a bank or a military post?"

"No, it's a school cafeteria office."

He laughed. "You're kidding me. What do you want to know? What's the next week's menu? When pizza day is coming up? Or maybe how much the soda machines are making."

"I don't know what's on there, and I don't want to know. I just need to get the files to the right people."

"And would that be the food police?" He laughed again. He was obviously enjoying this.

"Pretty close," I said. "But can you do it?" I asked.

"The U.S. Marines have a saying. The difficult we do right away; the impossible takes a little longer. This you can have right away."

"Great," I said.

"Here's what I need: the Internet provider. That would probably be for the whole school system. By the way where is this?"

"I have no idea," I said.

"Wow, this is real spook stuff," he replied. "Also I will need the specific computer number and the user ID and password. Can you get me that stuff?"

"I'll have to."

"What I'm going to do is create a mirror. It's called a mirror because it's a program that lets me see what is on another computer when it's operating. It's like having a mirror you look into and see something behind you. Someone will have to turn the computer on. Then I'll attach a mirror to the school computer's hard drive, and I'll be able to see what's on it here on my set up. Then we'll hack into the files and open the documents. Finally, I'll download all the files and send them to you immediately. I will erase them from my hard drive, and I suggest you do so as well, and as quickly as you can. Then I back out, and no one is the wiser. Piece of cake."

"I'll have a bite," I said.

Now I had to get to RJ and figure out a way to explain what had to be done. I went back to Facebook and sent him a message.

"Sam, it's Luke. Need to talk." He wasn't on. I would have to wait.

Mama came home from work and came into my room.

"You got that homework done?"

"Of course, Mama."

"Never doubted it," she said.

"You're a good boy, Lamar." She came over and gave me a hug. The books on the bed fell to the floor.

"Sorry, honey, I'll get them."

"No, Mama, you go to bed." She smiled at me and left my room, closing the door. I was a very lucky guy.

I played some games and read a little. I could hear Mama snoring, and I was getting tired. I went to turn off the computer when I saw a message from RJ.

"Luke, I'm here. Let's chat."

"Hey, Sam. Glad you got back to me. The doctor was happy to get that package."

"Good. Any ideas about my other thing."

"Yes. Let's see if I remember. I need the number of the package and the name and address. And I need to know its location." I was hoping he understood.

"Number?" he asked.

"Yes," I replied. "Every package has its own number."

"Oh, OK. I've got the name but what about the address?"

"Oh," I said. "It's just some letters and maybe a number."

"Oh, yes. I have that."

"One thing, Sam. You need to be with the package."

"That could be a problem."

"Doesn't work without it," I said.

RJ was quiet.

Then he replied, "I'll work on it. I'll send you the day and time as soon as I can."

"Be safe," I said and signed off.

CHAPTER FORTY-THREE

SATURDAY, MAY 7
RJ

After chatting with Lamar, I was worried. I got the part about the user ID and password. I also figured the location meant the school. That was easy. But I wasn't sure what he meant by the number.

But that wasn't the worst. He had said I needed to be with the computer. How was I going to pull that off? And do it without Becky. She was the one who saved me last time. I had to call Ryan.

"Sorry to bother you, but I need some help."

"Always here for you, big guy."

"I need to get some information to one of our friends, and I don't know what it is."

"Tell me," he said.

"He told me I needed the number of the computer we used to get information from. He says they all have numbers. What does he mean?"

"OK. They all have numbers. Any place with several computers that work together all have numbers. You can check it out yourself. Maybe your teacher can help you."

"Maybe. I'll give it a try."

"Are you all right, RJ? You don't sound so good."

"I'll be fine," I said. I hoped I was right.

On Monday, I had computer class with Ms. Arnold. She's an aide who helps us with the computers when we have work to do. I like her a lot. She always smiles at me and asks about my mom. Her kids are grown so she considers all of us her kids. I knew she was old because her hair was gray and she was very overweight and had trouble walking. Becky likes her too, and she told me Ms. Arnold has diabetes. I remember obesity was linked to diabetes. Becky said she heard the doctor might have to amputate one of her legs because of the disease. That made me angry and sad. I wondered if the food she ate caused her diabetes. I knew I had to keep helping this cause—for her and the kids in school.

Ms. Arnold has a very cool iPad. I want one. She has let me use it when I didn't have work. I was sitting at my station thinking about how and when I was going to get into the cafeteria office, when Ms. Arnold stopped and asked if she could help. She was holding the iPad, and I noticed a number on the back. It was stuck on with one of those plastic strips people use to put names on their toys or bikes. It was 01.22.002.003.

"What's that number on the back of your iPad?" I asked.

She turned it over and looked. "Oh this? It's called an IP address. It's the way the school keeps track of computers. They all have numbers. In fact, every time you print something or send an e-mail, the number of the computer is printed. That way, the school knows which computers are used for different things."

I had my answer.

When I got home that afternoon, I looked on one of the memos we had taken from the cafeteria. In the lower left-hand corner of the page was a number.

I left a message for Lamar on Facebook.

It said: "Luke, here's the info you need: topchef, potatochip, and 01.22.002.012. BTW the address is Blalock Middle School, Blalock, TN. Hope this is helpful. I'll have to get back to you about that date you asked for."

I still did not know how and when I was getting in the cafeteria alone.

CHAPTER FORTY-FOUR

MONDAY, MAY 9
LAMAR

When I got home from school on Monday, I checked my Facebook account right away. I had two messages. One was from RJ with all the things I needed to give to the Guardian. But he didn't have a date when he could be at the computer to turn it on so we could collect the data from the hard drive. I knew he was worried about that part, and I didn't want to push him. I was going to relay the information to the Guardian when I remembered the other message. It was from Dr. A.

"Luke, those letters you sent me were great. I want to be able to let other people see them. But before I do, we need to talk. When can I reach you?"

I typed back, "I am OK right now and will be for the afternoon and evening. I will turn on Skype. But at 5:30, it gets a little busy here, so talking would be tough."

I started my homework and forgot about 8th Day for a while.

About an hour later, I heard the Skype phone ring. It was Dr. A. so I accepted the call. The screen showed an empty chair, but I heard a voice.

"Lamar, congratulations. This material you sent is going to be a beginning in making changes in this country."

"Thank you," I said, "but this was really RJ's work. He's the one who took the chances."

"Of course, you're right," he said. "But we're all taking chances. And you always need to be careful. That's why evidence of this conversation will disappear when we're done."

"Sure," I said. "I get it." But I did think RJ was taking more chances.

"Let me tell you what we need. This information from RJ is perfect, but it's only from one place. We need to do more, for two reasons. First, we need to show that other schools are doing what Blalock is doing. Second, if we released this about Blalock, people would look for a leak, which would be dangerous for RJ."

"Do you think someone would actually hurt RJ?" I asked.

"Not physically, no. But there could be terrible repercussions, like his mom might lose her job, they could lose their house, or officials could accuse RJ of stealing school files. None of that will happen if we follow our own rules," he explained.

"I understand," I said. I would have to be very careful even around the Guardian.

"So," he continued, "we need this kind of information from many other schools. And because we don't have people in other schools like you and RJ, we have to do it electronically. I am going to send you a list of about fifty schools around the country. I will include all the passwords and ID usernames you will need to get into the schools' computers."

"But wait," I interrupted, "don't you need the computer on in order to get the information?" I knew the Guardian was right about that part.

"Yes, of course," he said, "but the school computers are on most of the day and some all day. What we want you to do is fish. That is, search each computer using key words connected to the papers we have from TN. When you get a hit, you will need to copy the file. Most schools are sloppy about security, and they are easily accessed. In addition, unless the files are encrypted, there will be no way to stop you from copying the data. If they were encrypted, then you would need special training to break the codes, and I am assuming that is not something you know how to do."

"You are assuming correctly."

"This will not be easy," he said. "You will have to do one school at a time and monitor what you find. Some places will have nothing or they will have a system you can't access. Whenever you are denied, immediately shut down so they can't trace you. But you probably know more about this than I do. I will leave it to you to figure it out. Just take your time, be careful, and remember to destroy any evidence that could be connected to you. Have you got it?"

"Yes, I think so."

"Good, I will start downloading the information to your hard drive now. Good luck and be safe."

Then he was gone.

CHAPTER FORTY-FIVE

MONDAY, MAY 9
LAMAR

This was one big deal. Dr. A. said he wasn't in a hurry, which was good because if I had to do it by myself, it would take days. Even though I knew I could do it alone, I also knew that I wasn't alone.

I went to Skype and punched in the Guardian's number. I heard the ringing. He accepted.

"Ahhh, it's the geekster. Looking for some company?"

"That would be nice," I said. "But I think I'll be getting too much soon. Mama and Jeane will be home before long. Could we talk later, like one in the morning?"

"Yeah, that would work. Call me and I'll be ready. Until then, I am off to protect the U.S. of A."

He was gone.

After dinner, I worked on my homework and Jeane and Mama watched TV. They were both off to bed by ten o'clock, and I said good-night and went to my room. I lay in bed for hours, thinking about what Karstan and Gracie were doing. I knew more about RJ than anyone else, and it seemed to me he was doing the bulk of the work, but I really didn't know. They could be working on important things I didn't know about. That was the point though, to keep us separated enough that no one person knew too much.

In my role, I was likely to know more about what they were doing, but they were the ones who were out there taking the chances. I was a little envious, but we all had parts to play. I must have dozed off, because I was surprised to hear a ring tone come from my computer. It wasn't loud, but it got my attention. I had signed on to Skype and kept my computer active so the Guardian could reach me at any time. I had set the sound low so no one would wake up if he called me first.

I shook my head, stumbled to the computer, and accepted his call.

"Taking a little nap, buddy?" he asked.

"I nodded off," I said.

"Are we going to do that school stuff you asked about?"

"Yes and no," I said. "Yes, it's school stuff, but no it's not what we talked about. The date for the job we discussed hasn't been set; the person there needs to get back to me about when he can do it. But I have another assignment and could use your help. I think I could do this by myself, but not with the speed you can."

"No flattery," he said, "until after I make it look easy."

"Here's the deal, we have a set of memos and e-mails from a school in Tennessee. These are memos about cafeteria business that I am working on. I need to verify the information in the memos is the same for schools throughout the country. I have a list of seventy-five schools from every region. We need to get into their computers and search for similar memos. I know we can do it with a program that will search for specific words used in the Tennessee memos. So I need you to write the program, help me go through these schools, and hopefully, find the information. Then we download and copy the memos. Can you help with this?"

He was silent for a minute.

"Of course I can do it, but I am worried about you. These memos don't sound like much. So why the secrecy?"

I was afraid I was going to lose him.

"You have to trust me on this," I said. "I am part of an important project collecting information to help school kids across the country. If I told you any more, I would break a promise I made when I joined the team. Trust me, this is important."

Another pause.

"OK," he said. "I can do this, but I want your word that you won't put yourself in trouble or talk about me."

"You have my word."

"OK, then let's get started. I want to explain to you how this will be done—you probably figured most of it out yourself—and then we will do it together. That way, you can let me know if you're getting what you need, and I'll know you are safe. Because if anything goes wrong, I'm going to burn our bridge so no one can trace this back to you. Are you good with that?"

"I'm good," I replied. Then he and I walked through the process. He needed time to get set up, so I gave him the school names and addresses, and we picked Wednesday night for the work.

CHAPTER FORTY-SIX

WEDNESDAY, MAY 11
RJ

When I got to school that morning, I wanted to talk to Becky about the science project. She was in homeroom chatting with her friends. She saw me come in and nodded. I sat down and got ready for the day. Mr. Kohla hadn't arrived yet. He was probably in the teacher's workroom getting ready. He was giving us a list of all the science projects and where they'd be located in the gym. The fair was set for Friday the twentieth, and he wanted to check in with us about our projects. We were covered on that front.

Becky came over to my desk.

"So are you ready for this?" she asked.

"Ready?" I asked back.

"Yeah, ready to tell The Bear about the project."

"Oh, that."

"You still upset about us not being straight with him?" she asked.

And other people, too, I thought. I sighed. "Yes," I admitted.

"Me, too," she said.

That surprised me. She didn't seem worried about anything we'd done or were about to do.

"You are?"

"Yeah," she said. "Surprised? I am too. I mean I like The Bear. I know he won't get in trouble because I plan on making sure everyone knows he didn't do anything. But he will be embarrassed, and I don't like that."

"Me neither," I said.

"My dad and I talk sometimes about ethics. And it's always complicated."

"What do you mean ethics?" I asked.

"Well, it's like what's right and wrong and what you should think about before doing something important."

"So how does that relate to what we're doing?" I asked.

"I don't know. It's complicated. We're doing a good thing helping kids be healthier, but we are not being completely honest about it. I don't include the witches in this because I don't like them, but my dad would say my not liking them should not matter. I wish I could ask him about it, but I'm afraid he might stop us, and I think we should keep going. Do you understand?"

More than you know, I thought. "I think so," I said. "I don't like it either, but it is important. If the adults were doing the right things, we wouldn't have to do uncomfortable things."

"My dad would call that rationalizing. That's making up a reason for doing something you know is wrong. He'd say you have to do what you think is right, and take the consequences of your actions."

"I understand that, but it's hard to tell what's right sometimes."

"It's interesting," she said. "Remember all we went through to get in the witch's office?"

"Sure."

"We probably didn't even have to go though all that. One of my dad's students was telling me the school is left open on the week-ends a lot. The door to the gym, which should lock when it closes, doesn't get locked. It's so old it doesn't close all the way and most times all you have to do is give it a jerk and it opens."

"OK, guys, time for the Pledge and announcements," Mr. Kohla said.

I didn't hear the announcements; I was thinking about the gym door.

CHAPTER FORTY-SEVEN

WEDNESDAY, MAY 11
LAMAR

Summer vacation was only a month away, but I didn't feel excited like I usually do. It meant days at the neighborhood pool, cookouts in the back yard, going to the youth center where I met with other guys who loved computers, and playing games for hours. No, instead I was thinking about two things: making sure I did my schoolwork to keep my perfect streak of all A's and taking care of the 8th Day stuff. And 8th Day was top priority. Today I got a message from RJ saying he was going to be at the computer on Saturday morning at eleven o'clock. I wasn't sure how we were going to work that out. But, tonight was the night the Guardian and I were going to collect the data from those middle schools across the country. I was excited and a little scared.

The day seemed to drag on forever. I stayed busy in school, and when I got home I worked on the end-of-year projects I had in four classes. After dinner I watched TV with Mama and Jeane, but I couldn't tell you what I saw. Then at nine it was time for bed. Mama kissed me good-night, and when I heard her go in her room, I set up Skype. The Guardian would call me at midnight.

I got in bed and read with my night-light. This time I would not fall asleep. And I didn't. I was sitting at the computer at midnight. I wanted to respond immediately to the ring so no one else would hear it. I accepted the call immediately.

The screen opened and there was the Guardian's room. Even by his standards, it was messy.

"OK, Tonto, you and the Lone Ranger are about to catch the bank robbers and save the day."

"What?" I said.

"Man," he said. "You should spend some quality time watching TV-land."

"Sure," I said. "Are you ready?"

"Born ready," he answered. "I've got the program up and running. We can start whenever you want. The program will target one school at a time in the order you gave me. It will open up the school and search for anything with the parameters we set for the key words: cafeteria, soda machines, school lunch programs, etc. If the computer system is off, it will move along to the next school. If the program doesn't find anything we are looking for, it will, again, move along. If it finds what we want, it will list the items and ask if we want copies. That's where you come in and let me know. I've set it up so you can see it running on your computer. Just go to the applications file and look for Tonto—that's you—and click on it."

I did. There was an open form with the name of the first school on it. There were also several empty spaces below with headings like on/off, data, yes/no, and copy. Those I understood. The last box's heading was "kill."

"What's this kill option?" I asked.

"Oooooh, that's the scary one," he said.

"Don't mess around with me, please."

"Not to worry. That's just there if I detect someone monitoring us or trying to ID us. Never gonna happen. But if it did, we would shut down immediately. You would close up, and I would get back to you when it was safe. But these are just schools, not the Pentagon or Federal Reserve."

"OK, I'm cool," I said, but that wasn't entirely true.

"Blast off," he said, "to infinity and beyond."

The program in front of me started to move. The first five schools were open and had several files that fit the criteria, and we copied them. The sixth school was not open; we skipped it. This all took less then five minutes.

Almost an hour later, we had fifty-three schools out of the seventy-five that were open and had material we wanted. Nineteen were of no help or not accessible. The seventy-third school was listed as Oak Ridge Tennessee Middle School. For some reason the program started to slow down. It was a full two minutes and nothing but the school's name was showing.

"This is strange," I heard the Guardian say.

"What do you mean str..." I didn't get to finish. A red light blinked in the kill area.

"OUT, RIGHT NOW," yelled the Guardian. The Skype connection ended, and I was looking at my home page. I was just starring when I realized I needed to close down.

I did. What had happened? I was afraid I was going to hear the phone ring or a knock at the door.

CHAPTER FORTY-EIGHT

THURSDAY, MAY 12
LAMAR

I sat still. Sweat was poring down my face. My heart was beating faster than I had ever felt it. I felt alone. Scared. Stupid. What had I done wrong? What was going to happen? Would Mama find out? Would Rashon and Jeane be in trouble? If the police asked me questions, what would I say? Was the Guardian going to prison? I worried about him the most. He was my friend. He was only trying to help me. It was my fault.

My computer started to ring; it was Skype. It was the Guardian. At least I hoped it was. The screen opened and there was his room.

"Do you know what's in Oak Ridge, Tennessee?" he asked. His voice was calm, but he wasn't joking around anymore.

"No," I said.

"Well, here's the history lesson," he started. "During World War Two...you have studied World War Two haven't you?"

"Of course."

"Well during the war, there was a race between the Allies, the good guys—that was us—and the Axis, the bad guys, Hitler and all that. They were racing to create the most destructive weapon and win the war. That weapon was the atomic bomb. The US knew it was a race our nation could not afford to lose, so *the* best scientists worked on the project. It was so secret that most people working on it didn't know what the other people working on it were doing. Make sense?"

"In fact, it does."

"OK. These scientists were working in three places so the enemy couldn't attack one location. Each place was responsible for different parts of the bomb work. One was in New Mexico, one was in Chicago, and guess where the other one was."

"Oak Ridge."

"Give that man a big panda bear. He wins the prize." He sounded a little more like himself. "Yes, my friend, Oak Ridge. And guess which site is still operating atomic research right now. And guess which place has a military presence to guard the place. Yes, you guessed it: Oak Ridge."

"So, are we dead?" I asked.

"No, my lucky friend, we are not, mostly because your friend, the genius, took precautions. Not that I was thinking about something as big as this."

"What happened?"

"My best guess is that with the new worry about terrorists, Oak Ridge Facility is locked down. And my second guess is that they have listeners—not unlike me—who pay attention to any attempts to break into their computers, and they most certainly include the town and school computers in their guarded area. So when we tiptoed in, we hit a trip wire, and they knew someone had come a-sneaking. But with my program alert, I knew immediately when they heard us and started to listen. That's what the kill switch was for. And that's what saved us."

"So they don't know it was us?"

"Very doubtful. If they did, they would have called us by now. They also would have shut down our computers, and they haven't. So they didn't have enough time to figure who we are. But guess what, we're not giving them another chance. In fact, I think you probably have enough information already. Don't you agree?"

"Absolutely," I said. "Sorry I got you into this."

"No sweat, man. I signed on. And actually this is more fun than anything I've done for the government guys in their suits."

"Thanks. I'm going to copy the files I have and send them off right now. Then I'll erase all of the evidence."

"Smart boy. I have already done that from this end. So, we're good?" he asked.

"We are," I said. Then I remembered. Oh, that other issue we talked about. Can you do it on Saturday at eleven?"

"No problem. Should be a walk in the park compared to this." He signed off.

I hoped that park didn't have any FBI agents hanging around.

CHAPTER FORTY-NINE

THURSDAY, MAY 12

THE NEW YORK TIMES

"POSSIBLE TERRORIST BREAK-IN ATTEMPT"

Early this morning, a source told a *Times* reporter that a federal agent had foiled an attempt to break in to Oak Ridge Tennessee's computer system. Sometime after midnight this morning, an alarm went off in the headquarters of the Oak Ridge Security Division. An agent assigned to listen in on all traffic immediately began a back trace to ascertain the origin of the breach. Reporters were told that the party or parties attempting the break-in went off-line too quickly to be traced.

The Oak Ridge facility has been used for testing and evaluating nuclear fission since the Second World War. The facility remains a top-secret asset. The military and civilian leaders of the facility declined to elaborate on what those responsible for the break-in might have been looking for.

General Thomas Belden said, "We continue to be vigilant. This facility is a prime target for those who would do this nation harm. Accordingly, every possible safe guard is present."

The White House had no comment.

CHAPTER FIFTY

WEDNESDAY, MAY 11
KARSTAN

I couldn't believe it would take so long to be alone. It had been two weeks, and every night either Mom or Dad had been home. And when they weren't around, Carmella was. And for some reason, Carmella seemed to be watching me. I never noticed that before. Go figure. It was probably just paranoia. Finally I had a night by myself. Mom had called to say she couldn't be home before nine, and Dad had called after her to let me know he had to stay late at the hospital to watch over a patient who had had complications during surgery. They each thought the other would be home.

I went up to Mom's computer and I turned it on. I found her documents; there were dozens of folders, each with a name attached. They appeared to be the names of the companies and people Mom's law firm worked for. I looked at each name and recognized some of the people as friends of my parents or people I heard them talking about at dinner sometimes. Some of the companies were easy; they were places where the parents of some of my friends from school worked. I looked at a couple of those, hoping to find something exciting, but I didn't. It was all lawyer talk and made no sense.

There, near the end of the list, was AgraInc. That was the name Uncle Jerry had mentioned. I opened the file. It was enormous. There were over thirty subfolders, each with another title. I didn't know where to start, so I just started to open them one at a time. The first one I opened was named Commercial Production. When I opened it my mouth dropped open. There were 1,032 documents.

I opened the first one; it was fifty-five pages long. I started reading. It was all about profit margins, weather, projected outcomes, overseas markets, personnel issues, and government regulations. It might as well have been written in another language. I knew nothing.

I had already spent an hour looking at the files when I realized it was a waste of time. If I had a week alone, I don't think I could have gone through all the documents, and even if I did, I wasn't sure I would know if I came across anything important.

It was clearly time for me to contact the kid who was our computer guy. Lamar. He had set up Facebook accounts for us. So I knew how to reach him. I could do that on my own computer.

I heard the door close.

"Karstan, I'm home," my Dad said. I heard him open the refrigerator, but I knew I didn't have much time.

"Be right down, Dad," I said.

"I hope you've eaten," he said.

"Of course, Dad."

I was closing myself out of the document I had been reading and was just about to get out of AgraInc when I saw a file named SchoolMeals. That was the subsidiary Uncle Jerry had mentioned.

I wanted to open it, but I heard Dad start up the stairs. I shut the program, turned the computer off, and went to the door. He wasn't around the corner of the stairwell, so I walked quickly to my room and took a deep breath.

CHAPTER FIFTY-ONE

THURSDAY, MAY 12
LAMAR

I was exhausted all day in school, but at the same time there was a feeling of excitement. I had peeked at the documents we had gotten from all those schools. Even though I hadn't had time to read very many, it was clear even to me that they all looked very similar to the ones RJ had gotten from his school. I wasn't sure what to make of it, but I knew what I had to do. Using all my energy, I got through school and went home. I was alone for at least an hour before Jeane came in. I immediately logged on to Facebook and left a message for Dr. A.

"Beard, I was wondering if you had those stories I sent you. I thought they were pretty funny. Talk to me when you can. Luke."

I sat back and did some homework while I waited. I wondered how RJ was going to get to that computer on Saturday. I hoped he was safe. In fact, I hoped everyone was safe. When I agreed to do this, I knew it might be hard, but I couldn't see the danger I guessed we all were facing. I realized if one of us got caught not much would happen to us since we were minors. And none of us could implicate the other members because we didn't know each other's full names or location. Correction, I had a pretty good idea where RJ lived, but I had erased all evidence of that, and I wouldn't tell. Or so I told myself. I was pretty tough when no one was around. Mostly I was afraid if Mama found out, she would be ashamed of me. But Jeane said this was important, and I would trust her about anything. She has helped Mama take care of me after Dad died, and I know she wouldn't put me at risk. Not that I would tell on her or Rashon either, but I suspect Jeane would take responsibility for all of it. I just didn't want it to come to that.

I glanced at the computer. Dr. A. had posted a message.

"Luke, yes, they were hilarious. I loved them. You tell a great story. In fact I can guarantee quite a few people will be hearing these stories. They are too good not to pass on."

"Thanks. There's another part I will tell you later. But I also wanted you to know Sam's family issue is coming up soon."

"And does he have the help he needs?"

"Yes."

"Well, good."

"In fact, I should be able to let you know how it works out this Saturday."

"I look forward to it."

We closed Facebook. I hoped Dr. A would approve of what RJ and I were doing; everything was happening so fast. I thought about it and decided it would be too hard to stop everything at this point.

I needed to check in with the Guardian, but that would have to wait until after dinner. Mama would be home soon.

After dinner I said I needed to work on a report, which was true, so I went to my room. I was busy with schoolwork for several hours before Mama came in and said good-night.

I waited another fifteen minutes to call the Guardian.

He answered almost immediately.

"Is this going to be more trouble?" he asked.

"I certainly hope not. But I wanted to be sure we were set for Saturday at eleven."

"I wanted to talk to you about that."

Oh, no, I thought. *He's going to back out. I almost wouldn't mind if I knew I could stop RJ.*

"You don't want to do it?" I asked.

"No, I do want to help, but I have been thinking about what almost happened the last time."

"I understand," I said. "If we can't, we can't."

"Oh, we can all right, but I have some rules. If you can't follow them, then I'm out."

"OK, what are they?"

"Pretty simple actually. First, you need to use another computer than your own. Second, choose a very public computer, so if someone traces us, they'll have nowhere to go. Finally, when we're done, you get out of there right away and go home. I will see you on Skype and show you what we've got. Then we can work out what to do with it. *Capiche?*"

"What?"

"Do you understand?" he asked.

"Yes."

"And can you assure me that you can do those things? Because I will know in a minute if you do not."

I had to think. I couldn't lie to this guy; he had been too good to me. I knew Rashon would be the key. If he could set me up, then it would work.

"I can assure you that I can do it. And if I cannot, I will end it immediately. Is that OK?"

"Yes, I trust you."

"Then we're on."

CHAPTER FIFTY-TWO

FRIDAY, MAY 13
NBC NEWS, NEW YORK
THE EVENING NEWS

"Finally, our last story of the night. Major American newspapers released internal documents and e-mails from schools across the country this morning. What the documents had in common may surprise you. All of them dealt with school lunches. Here is Sean Bernard, our investigative reporter, at one of those schools. Sean?"

"Thanks, Celia. I'm standing in front of DeWitt Clinton Middle School here in Manhattan. *The New York Times, The Boston Globe, The San Francisco Examiner,* and papers in almost every major city in the country published documents from forty-five middle schools in various locations: the Northeast, the South, the Midwest, and the West Coast. I am standing in front of one of those schools.

"All the documents were similar, although not identical. The common thread running through them was information that suggested the schools were running lunch programs that were not providing the best possible lunches for our kids. There were comments about needing to consider the finances of the program even if the programs were substandard. In addition, there were details of schools using cookies to fulfill the grain requirements and apple tarts being used for fruit requirements. Not since the Reagan administration sought to have ketchup designated as a vegetable, have these types of substitutions been mentioned. In addition, there was information of the money provided by soft drink companies to have their products available to the kids. Here are some direct quotes from the documents. Remember, the documents came from more than three-dozen schools nationwide. I will not use the name of any school, but I will say the quotes I read are verbatim and appear in most of the memos from the majority of schools.

"First: Kola-King has a long tradition of being committed to education. Our company will be happy to help your schools with funding for technology equipment, scoreboards, supplies, and other needs. In addition we will profit share with your schools in the use of our food and beverage vending machines.

"Second: SharpCo is proud to provide your school with both soft drink and snack vending machines. As a result of this partnership we are happy to provide the school with supplies and/or devices that will aid in the school's mission.

"Finally, this information appeared as memos from state agencies to local school districts. The wording differed but the content was essentially the same as the one I will read: Congratulations! Food preparation choices in your school lunches such as cookies serving as a grain product and french fries serving as a vegetable product have increased income by over 35 percent. In addition, minimizing food choices and maximizing food reutilization has decreased costs by almost 50 percent.

"Actually, Celia, I'm not exactly sure what that last sentence means. Our researchers here at NBC have shared these statistics with me. School vending machines are found in 97 percent of our nation's high schools and 82 percent of middle schools. Reports from nutritional experts say 75 percent of these beverages and snacks would be classified as unhealthy.

"I tried to talk to Principal Suarez at the end of school today. I caught up with her as she watched over dismissal. Let's go to the tape."

"Principal Suarez, Principal Suarez, can you tell us about these memos and documents?"

"I have no comment."

"But is it true the school menus do not reflect what should be served?"

"As I said, no comment."

"Well can you tell us if this document I have here, which has your school seal and your name on it, is real?"

"No more questions. You need to talk to the school board about this."

"Well, Cecilia, as you can see, I didn't get very far. And calls to the school board have not been returned."

"Sean, can you tell me if these papers have been authenticated?"

"No, Cecilia, I cannot, but all the newspaper reports indicate that none of the schools named would deny anything. The newspapers indicate they received the material from an unnamed source, and when they tried to validate the information, the named schools would not cooperate. Each paper made efforts to give the schools a chance to dispute the details, but they refused to do so. We'll see what happens from here, Cecilia."

"Thanks, Sean. There has been some speculation that the information came from the group 8th Day. 8th Day is an organization—

some call it a radical organization—that has been calling for national investigations into the health of American children, particularly in regards to nutrition. They assert that the government is not paying attention to what they call a crisis of epic proportions. Dr. Ralph Oteri, a biology professor at Columbia University, heads the group. Dr. Oteri specializes in nutrition. But the organization claims thousands of members across the country, many of them professors and college students. In a phone conversation with me today, Dr. Oteri said that to his knowledge his organization had nothing to do with this leak, but added he was happy the public had evidence of what his group has been saying: our children are in danger.

"We will be watching this story closely. There is nothing I can think of that is more important than the health of our children. Good-night from New York."

CHAPTER FIFTY-THREE

FRIDAY, MAY 13
KARSTAN

It was Friday night and mom and dad had gone to Rolling Hills, our country club, for dinner with friends. Carmella had made some dinner for me. She is a great cook, and I love her food. I was eating in the kitchen, watching the TV next to the refrigerator when Mom and Dad came down.

"Is dinner good?" Mom asked.

"Great," I replied.

"Doesn't your mom look lovely?" Dad asked.

"Of course," I said. She did look nice. Her hair was loose around her face unlike the pulled back way she wears it to work. She had on a red dress and wore a gold necklace.

"Well, your old man doesn't look so bad either," Mom said.

"He's OK," I answered.

"Thanks, buddy."

"Welcome," I said, but I was watching the TV.

Mom said, "Now we'll be home by midnight, but I expect you to be in bed by then. You have the club's number, so call if you need us."

"K." I said. Then they left.

I waited for an hour watching TV. When I was sure Mom and Dad weren't coming home for something, I went upstairs to my room. I opened my computer and went to Facebook. My pseudonym is Carl Shultz, and I'm an engineer from New Jersey. I thought it sounded pretty lame, but no one would guess it was me. I sent a message to Lamar, aka Luke. I told him I wanted to talk and to get back to me soon. I didn't know anything, really, about the School-Meals folder, other than Uncle Jerry mentioned it. So I thought I should pass it on.

I turned on the TV in my room and watched some awful show that was supposed to be funny but wasn't. I kept an eye on the computer to see if someone came up on chat.

About half an hour later, someone did. It was Lamar/Luke.

"Hi, Carl. How's the weather in New Jersey?"

I didn't know if I could keep up this silly spy stuff, but I answered, "OK. Look I have this thing I need help with. I know it should be easy, but I can't work it out."

"Tell me about it," he said.

"Well..." I had to think about how to explain the situation. "I have this a...project at work. I have the...plans on one computer, and I need to send them to my boss. The information is technical and very long, and I don't want to screw up. Can you walk me through this."

"Sure," he replied. "In fact, I can send it to your boss if you want. I think I have his address."

"Yeah, that would be great. So what do I do?"

"Is it on the computer you're using?"

"No, it's in another room."

"That's fine. Go to the other computer and load up."

"Give me a few minutes." I went to my mother's computer and logged on. I went right to the folder titled SchoolMeals. "OK, I've got the folder."

"Fine. Send an e-mail with the files from the folder as attachments to your other computer. Do you know how to do that?" he asked.

"Yes, even I can do that." I didn't know what we were doing, but I e-mailed it.

"Done," I wrote back.

"Good. This helps with security and always makes a backup available."

In code that meant it would help me not get caught. So, Lamar was smart. I liked that.

"Now go to the other computer and forward that e-mail with the attachments to me."

"Give me another minute," I said. I closed my Mom's computer and went to mine. I found the e-mail and forwarded it to Lamar.

"So when will my boss get this?" I asked.

"I just sent it. He should have it by now," Lamar said.

"That's great. Thanks a lot. I hope my boss likes it."

"I'm sure he will. And by the way, I would delete the e-mail now, so your report isn't hanging around cyber space."

"Good thinking," I answered.

We left Facebook. I wondered if I would ever know what happened to the stuff.

CHAPTER FIFTY-FOUR

SATURDAY, MAY 14
RJ

Mom left for her restaurant job at Shenanigan's at nine o'clock. I figured that would give me plenty of time to get to the cafeteria and be ready at eleven. I had my cell phone with me. Lamar and I had agreed to take a chance and use cell phones because we didn't know how else to pull this off.

I left the house and walked slowly down the street toward the school. I was hoping not to see anyone, but it was Saturday morning and people were on the street going to the post office and shopping. I said hello to the people I knew but hoped they would forget they saw me.

I went past the school and into the yard of a law office I knew was closed. I went in the backyard and walked back to the school. The playground was empty and I crossed it, keeping my eyes open for anything or anyone. I saw no one. I got behind the building and walked past the loading area that backed up to the cafeteria. Around the corner was the gym. Again I looked around. There was a whole line of old oaks and maples that blocked the property next to the school from seeing and sometimes hearing all the kids. Today it was quiet. The gym was built on an area slightly lower than the front of the school, so I couldn't see the street, and no one on the street could see me.

The door was in the center of the gym wall. There were windows high up on the wall so light could come in the gym. During the winter kids played basketball games in there, but nothing today—I hoped.

I walked up to the door and looked around again. Nothing. I grabbed the handle and gave it a yank upward. It didn't open. I felt light-headed. If I couldn't get in, I was letting many people down. I took a deep breath and yanked the handle up as hard as I could. I heard a small pop and the door leaned slightly open, making a creaking sound. I was sure someone heard it. I stood still for a minute, waiting for someone to come. Nobody did.

I pulled the door slowly open. It creaked again. I stopped. I would be here all afternoon if I didn't move. I grabbed the handle and pulled the door wide. It continued to creak, but I jumped inside and slammed it shut. I stood against the wall without breathing. I could feel my heart pounding in my chest. The light from the windows made the gym easy to see in.

When I heard nothing but my heart beating, I moved across the gym and went through the door into the corridor. I stopped. The darkened offices were on my left. They had windows that looked out on the corridor leading from the gym.

I saw no one and heard no one. I moved quickly past the wall of glass and came to the end of the corridor. There was a little entryway there that students used while waiting for buses and for parents when they came to school for presentations. I looked to the left, out the doorway leading to a parking lot. Again, no one was there. I quickly turned right onto the corridor going to the classrooms. In front of me, about twenty yards ahead, was the door to the library. I ran up to the door. Now I had to turn left and then right into the corridor with the windows all along the left side. The courtyard was empty, but I decided to take no chances.

I knelt over and ran the length of the corridor hoping I was under the windows and out of sight. I didn't stop until I was at the cafeteria door. I took the handle, opened the cafeteria door, and ran in. I stopped to take a breath. The cafeteria had no windows, and it was dark. I touched the side of the wall with my left hand and inched along. There was enough light coming from the door that I started to see tables and chairs stacked up in the far corner.

When I got to the door we had used before, I turned the handle slowly praying it was open. It was.

I entered the kitchen and tiptoed behind the preparation tables, watching out for hanging kitchen tools. I knew Mrs. Nunley's office was at the end of the kitchen. When I reached it, I grasped the handle and opened the door.

I was in the office.

I closed the door and turned on my phone. It gave me just enough light to see the desk and computer. I checked the time. It was 10:55 a.m. I decided to call Lamar anyway. He answered on the first ring.

"I'm in," I said.

"Good, we are set on this end."

"We?"

"Don't ask. Just boot up and get to those documents."

I used the ID and password to get the computer going. It didn't make much noise, but it sounded loud to me.

"OK, I'm in," I said.

"Good," Lamar answered. "Now go to the document files."

"OK. But the trouble we had last time was there were too many; there must be a dozen document files."

"Not to worry," Lamar replied. He sounded very cool about the situation, and I wished I felt the same.

"We are going to copy them all," he continued. "Then when we have them all, we will open them and unencrypt them if necessary, and the boss will decide what is important."

"How are you going to do that," I asked.

"It would take too much time to explain. Just a minute," he paused. I heard him talking to someone.

"OK," he said to someone else. "Now, RJ, just look at the screen. You should see a small window open and then a copy bar appear."

"A copy bar?" I asked.

"Just that long blue line you see when you download."

"OK, I see it."

"Underneath it you will see numbers moving very fast as the files are copied. The copy bar will fill up with blue like a thermometer getting hotter. Got that?"

"Yes," I said, "I have downloaded before."

"So watch," Lamar said.

And I did. The numbers zoomed, and the bar turned bluer. In less then three minutes, the screen said, "done."

"Lamar," I said, "it's done."

"Yes, we know. Now you close that computer and get out of there." He hung up.

I didn't need any encouragement. I turned the computer off, turned my phone off, and backed my way out.

I moved faster than when I came in, and in no time I was closing the door to the gym. I wondered if I had even breathed during the last few minutes.

But it was OK. It was done and I was on my way home.

CHAPTER FIFTY-FIVE

SATURDAY, MAY 14
LAMAR

It had been an interesting morning. I told Rashon I needed access to and privacy at a computer. He wanted to ask why but did not. He told me the Wayne State library had private rooms, and he agreed to arrange for me to use one. He would have a friend meet me at the main desk and set me up in one of the rooms. He told me to look for a guy wearing a name tag with Ernest on it.

So I rode the bus to the university and went to the library. It was huge and I loved it. But I needed to focus, so I went to the main area. I approached the young girl working behind the desk and asked for Ernest. She called behind her to a glassed-in room.

"Ernest, there's someone to see you."

A tall, pale-skinned, skinny guy got up from his chair. He walked from behind the work area and started to make his way across the library. I hurried after him and finally caught up.

"I'm Lam..." I started to say.

He turned and looked at me, then turned away and kept walking.

"I don't know your name, and I don't want to know your name. We never met so we can't know each other," he said. "Clear?"

He turned and looked at me. He did not look happy.

"Yes," I said quietly.

He took me to the back of the big room and opened a door, which led to a long hallway. There were windows on the walls. We were passing rooms with computers, and in each room a few people were working at stations. We reached an empty room. He opened the door and we went in. There were probably thirty computers there. He took me to the farthest corner and pointed at a seat. I sat. I couldn't see the door and no one could see me from the windows.

"This is your spot. I'm going to lock the door from the outside; no one will be able to get in. When you're done, let yourself out and leave the door unlocked. When you leave don't look for me or at me. Clear?"

"Yes," I repeated.

He turned on the computer.

"I've signed you in. When you're done, be very, very sure you have turned every program and window off and then exit."

"Clear," I said. I thought he might smile, but he did not. He left and I got to work. I used Skype to let the Guardian know I was there.

"You ready, buddy?"

"I guess."

"Don't tell me where you are. Just go to myipaddress.com and tell me the number."

I read it to him.

"OK. Give me a minute and I'll get into your machine."

I waited.

"OK, I'm set. You should diminish the Skype page so you can hear me, but you will also see what we are getting. Now when we start loading, I'm going to let you watch. Then when we cut your friend loose, I want you to look at what we have. Then tell me what we need to keep and where you want it sent. I will take care of it. Got it?" he asked.

"Clear, " I said. This was getting weird even for me. My phone rang. It was RJ. He was ready; I told the Guardian. RJ asked who I was talking to, but I didn't want him to know.

The whole operation took maybe a half hour. RJ was done with his part in maybe ten minutes. I told him we were done and hung up.

"OK, champ, give me fifteen to twenty minutes to get this stuff so it makes sense to you, and then I'll let you see it."

He went to work and didn't say anything. Finally, I saw documents on my screen.

"There you have it. Start looking and deciding." There were about ten files. I eliminated seven because they were operating instructions for the cooking equipment in the cafeteria. The last three had some promise. One in particular looked important. It was titled "Biennial Report on School Lunch Program Effectiveness." I thought it best to send all three to Dr. A.

I explained my decision to the Guardian. He dumped the seven, and I gave him Dr. A's e-mail address for the remaining three.

"We done good, Red Ryder. All's been sent off to the mountain. Adios time. Be sure you clear everything from the computer," he reminded me.

"All ready been told that," I said.

"Happy trails then." And he was gone.

I cleaned up and headed home. It was almost one o'clock so I didn't have much time. I went on Facebook and looked to talk to Dr. A. He was already on.

"Been waiting for you, Luke," he said.

"Busy day," I said.

"I can imagine," he answered.

"So how are things?" I asked.

"Better than anything I expected," he assured me.

"I was hoping the report might be helpful," I replied.

"Along with what I got yesterday, it's a gold mine. Thanks to you and your friends. I'm off to see what gets done with this info."

He was gone.

CHAPTER FIFTY-SIX

SUNDAY, MAY 15
RJ

I slept soundly, better than any night of the past week. With the cafeteria caper out of the way, I felt like a huge rock had been lifted from my shoulders. I had no idea what was in those files, and I didn't know if they would be helpful, but I didn't care. I was done. I could get back to my normal life. I stayed in bed until almost ten o'clock. I heard mom in the kitchen, but she didn't call me.

Finally I got myself together enough to go downstairs.

"Well, there you are sleepyhead. Are you OK?"

"Couldn't be better," I said.

"Great, let me make you some breakfast. Would you like a bagel, or maybe a muffin?"

"Actually, Mom, I think I would like some oatmeal or some granola, if you have it," I replied.

"Well what's up with you? Has that science project got you thinking about what you eat?" she asked.

"As a matter of fact, it has," I said. "And today I have to get some work done before the science fair this Friday. Becky gave me a website to look at more than a week ago, and I haven't done my part."

"Oh, so this is really about Becky, isn't it? You like her don't you?" Mom asked.

"Mom," I started.

"Oh, I think she's cute," Mom cut me off. "And I know she's a good student. You should bring her over. I'd like to talk to her."

"Mom, just the breakfast. OK?" I said.

She smiled. "Of course. I think we have what you want. I bought it for Ryan when he was here, and I have plenty left over."

She made me breakfast and happily didn't bring up Becky again.

After eating, I went to my room and looked up schoollunchbox. org. It was an amazing site. There was a ton of information about healthy eating, specifically at lunchtime. In fact, the writers recommended bringing lunch to school unless you knew the school lunches were good enough.

They outlined what a school lunch should contain. I wasn't surprised to see their idea of a healthy lunch didn't match what our school offered. Their suggested choices from the protein group included lean meat or fish, cottage cheese, and eggs; but instead, we got corn dogs, ham subs, cheese sticks, and pizza. Healthy options from the fruit and vegetable group are fresh fruit, broccoli, green beans, strawberries, and apples. Our school served fruit pies, turnovers, cheesy green beans, applesauce, and onion rings. And we should eat a healthy grain with lunch too, like whole wheat bread, oatmeal bread, brown rice, corn, and peas. We had to choose from french fries and cookies. And instead of the recommended glass of milk, most kids drank juice or soda. The website says it is against the rules to drink soda and eat junk food in the cafeteria at lunch, but kids do it all the time.

I called Becky.

"Nice to hear from you, RJ. We haven't talked much in a while."

"My fault," I said. "I had some things to do. All done now. I just was looking at schollunchbox.org and it's great. I can see why you never eat our school lunches."

"No kidding," she said. "And here is the best part. It's going to make our project the best."

"How?" I asked.

"Simple," she said. "First we'll finish up the silly part. I've got the survey results, and I'll give them to you tomorrow. Most of the time the kids were honest, I think. Needless to say pizza was the favorite. But a lot of people talked about the vegetables they supposedly like and eat. I'll believe that when I see your notes on what they really eat."

"That will be tomorrow," I said. "I checked with Mr. Kohla, and I can sit at a table near the line and take notes. Last week he showed me where to sit and Mrs. Nunley..."

"The head witch," Becky interrupted.

"Yup. She came out and started telling me and Mr. Kohla that no way was I going to sit there and upset the kids."

"The only thing that upsets the kids is the junk she serves," said Becky.

"Well, Mr. Kohla went to the office and came back with Mrs. Reardon. I couldn't hear them talking, but it was obvious Mrs. Nunley was very angry. Mrs. Reardon didn't look happy either."

"She never does," said Becky.

"That's for sure. But when they were done, Mrs. Nunley left quickly making lots of noise. Mrs. Reardon walked out and gave me a nasty look. But Mr. Kohla came over and told me it was all set up. He also said I had your dad to thank for this."

"Way to go, Dad," Becky cheered. "Here's what I'm thinking: you get your information and I'll give you the survey. Then you can write up something about the survey and what we supposedly learned. I'm going to take our school menus and compare them to what schoollunchbox.org says we should be eating. I'll cite the references they use from the university and nutritionists. Then I'll write up a section on the comparison and how awful our lunches are. I'll let you see it as soon as I'm done. Plus I'll run it by my dad to see if he thinks it's OK to use."

"I like it," I replied. I couldn't believe I was saying that because not long ago I didn't want to do anything to upset the cafeteria people or Mrs. Reardon. But after I had seen how they acted, I didn't care anymore.

"So let's go to my house on Thursday after school, and we will put the information on the poster. Then we can decide who will answer the questions from the parents."

"Sounds fine," I said. "But let's meet here. My mom wants to meet you, and she gets home early Thursday."

"Oh," she said, "I get to meet the mother. What does this mean my friend?" She was laughing.

"Don't give me a hard time," I said and hung up.

Monday was the big day. I had a copy of Becky's Survey

SCHOOL LUNCH CHOICES SURVEY 1

Becky Albright

RJ Johnson

Eighth Grade Science Fair

Blalock Middle School

Please tell us what you eat from the school lunches each week.

What is your favorite drink from the school lunch?

> Milk
>
> Water
>
> Juice
>
> Soda

What is your favorite meat/meat alternative choice from the school lunch?

> Pizza
>
> Corn dog
>
> Ham hoagie
>
> Rib sandwich
>
> Cheese taco
>
> Chicken nuggets
>
> Grilled cheese

What is your favorite vegetable from the school lunch?

> Cheesy green beans
>
> Cheesy broccoli
>
> Salad
>
> Fried onion rings

What is your favorite grain from the school lunch

    Corn

    French fries

    Cookies

    Peas

What is your favorite fruit from the school lunch

    Fruit pie

    Fruit pop

    Fruit turnover

    Applesauce

At lunch time, I took my bag lunch, a notebook, and pen along with Becky's survey to the cafeteria. I sat at the table Mr. Kohla told me to use. While I waited for the kids to go though the line, Mrs. Nunley glared at me. I didn't look at her. All the ladies were scowling, except for Miss Sally who smiled at me and winked.

The information I got was pretty boring. The kids chose the stuff they said they liked, except, as Becky predicted, almost no one took the vegetables, even though they said they would. I watched twenty-eight kids for three days.

SCHOOL LUNCH: WHAT KIDS ACTUALLY EAT

Becky Albright
RJ Johnson
Eighth Grade Science Fair
Blalock Middle School

Watched twenty-eight kids for three days.

Monday

What did the kids actually drink?
Milk: 6
Water: 4
Juice: 11
Soda: 7 (brought them into the cafeteria, which is illegal)

How many kids chose the corn dog? 7

How many kids chose the salad? 3

How many kids chose the applesauce? 17

How many kids chose the cookies? 23

How many kids chose the french fries? 19

How many kids chose the fruit pie? 20

Number of kids who brought choices from the vending machines to the cafeteria (illegal)? 12

How many kids chose less than 3 of the groups offered (illegal)? 17

I spent much of the rest of the day thinking about what would happen when we set up our science fair project.

CHAPTER FIFTY-SEVEN

"And we're back. This is Sean Bernard with the "News of the Week." You will remember a series of school communications were leaked to the press last week in regards to the relationship between soft drink companies and public schools, and specifically the use of questionable menu items in our schools. At that time, I tried to get local education officials to comment on the memos. We were interested in the veracity of those memos and whether or not the schools indeed were substituting unhealthy food choices in place of acceptable menu items. As of today, despite many phone calls, no one in the school system has commented. What was particularly disturbing to me were the references indicating these food choices were made in order to save and/or make money for the school systems. The silence has been deafening. In fact, the only comments from the schools have been accusations that the memos were obtained illegally and should not have been published. I will speak for this station and tell you we have no idea where the leaks came from. The newspapers involved have indicated the memos were delivered anonymously. But the reporters who broke the story have acknowledged they checked the information and deemed it authentic. Although they will not release the names of the school personnel who vouched for the memos, they have made it clear they believe them to be genuine. It is interesting that although some school systems have called foul, none of them have flat out denied the truth of the released memos.

"Tonight I have a guest who has kindly agreed to talk to us about the situation, and we are grateful for his willingness to share his insight. He is Dr. Robert Bernstein. He works for a subsidiary of the large food company AgraInc. His division is school meals so we are pleased to have someone who is involved in the industry willing to talk with us."

"Thanks for being here, Dr. Bernstein."

"My pleasure, Sean."

"Let's start with the information about soft drink companies and their relationships with school systems. Does it seem like a conflict of interest to you that schools are inviting companies who make and deliver foods most nutritionists say are not appropriate for young people to eat and drink, or even older people for that matter?"

"Let me comment on that from several perspectives. First, I would argue the idea that these products are unhealthy is more opinion than fact. Second, I would point out that these products are available in stores and restaurants throughout the country, and they are very successful because the consumer wants them. This is a free market enterprise system and customers make choices. Finally, the school systems enter into these agreements voluntarily, and they profit from them in many ways."

"In what ways, Doctor?"

"Well, they supply revenue the schools use to purchase needed items such as supplies and technology."

"And football and basketball scoreboards with the companies' logos on them?" Sean asked.

"In some cases."

"Let me see if I have this correct," Sean replied. "You are saying the nutritional value of these drinks and snacks is a matter of opinion."

"Certainly," he responded.

"Well, are you aware that more than 95 percent of nutritionists in this country find these items to be harmful to young people?"

"There have been many studies of foods and food supplements over the last twenty years. The outcomes vary. And, as I said, these are choices people make."

"But your business specializes in school lunches," said Sean.

"Yes, as I have said," he responded.

"So you are saying that the kids choose."

"Of course they do, and by extension, their parents. If their parents don't want them to eat something, they should tell their children not to."

"But we don't count on the parents to simply tell their children not to smoke, do we?"

"That's completely different."

"I'm not so sure, but let's go on to something else. Do you believe, as these memos seem to indicate, that school systems are substituting poorer quality food in their school lunches in order to turn a profit?"

"I think it's more complicated than you make it sound," said the doctor.

"How so?" Sean asked.

"Schools, as you know, are dealing with difficult decisions because of budget cuts. And I think it's unfair to judge them without knowing all the facts."

"But it seems to me the health of their students should be their first concern. Don't you?"

"Of course, but as I said, it's complicated," replied the doctor. His tone of voice was patronizing.

"Yes, you have, and I get that," said Sean. "But let's move on." Sean picked up a stack of papers from the table beside him. "I have in my hands a report that is written every other year by the government. Its research deals with the quality of the school lunch programs nationally and, among other things, the rate of obesity in students. Are you familiar with this report?" asked Sean.

"Where did you get that?" asked the doctor who was now visibly angry.

"Ah," said Sean, "so I'll take that as authenticating this report."

"I'm not authenticating anything, and you shouldn't have it," said the doctor. Now he was angry.

"And yet I do," said Sean. "Tomorrow this report is likely to be in all the major papers in this country. Any comment?"

The doctor paled.

"You lied to me. I will not participate in this interview any longer. Our attorneys will take over from here." The doctor stood up and walked off the set.

"Well, unfortunately our guest has left me with two minutes to fill. Let me spend the time reading some excerpts from this report. For your information, SMI is School Meals Initiative.

All school food authorities participating in the National School Lunch Program must undergo an SMI review on a cyclical basis.

Results from this year's SMI report indicate that only 45 percent of the 2000 plus schools required by law to complete the survey actually did. The results from the schools that did as required by law indicate there is no change over the last decade when it comes to improving the National School Lunch Program.

"So as you just heard, no improvement in the last decade. Listen to the statistics.

Less than 8 percent of the schools involved in the review met the dietary guidelines for Americans.

"Yes, you heard me correctly, less than 8 percent. And there's more.Less than 30 percent of the schools involved in the review met the guidelines for the fat intake. Less than 7 percent of the schools involved in the survey met the guidelines for fiber intake. Less than 10 percent of the schools involved in the survey met the guidelines for sodium intake.

"It has also come to our attention that part of the SMI mandate does not require the data collectors to make this data available to the public unless directly required through legislation.

"What can I say, this is a travesty. Remember that The NAEP Report, more commonly known as the Nation's Report Card, is also done on a regular basis, and the results are reported in most newspapers across the country. So we know the school curriculum, but we don't know the health value of the lunch program. Amazing.

"I find this hard to believe, but here it is. I am guessing we will hear more about this.

"Thanks for watching."

CHAPTER FIFTY-EIGHT

THURSDAY, MAY 19
RJ AND BECKY

So Becky came over after school on Thursday. Mom wasn't home yet, but she would be by four. I had a chance to look at Becky's survey results. They were pretty much what we expected. Pizza and chicken nuggets were the big winners. The one surprising finding was how many students chose salad as a vegetable; it wasn't a majority, but there were at least twenty-five people out of the eighty-one who took the survey. Unfortunately, when I watched them at the lunch line, only three people of the twenty-eight chose the salad. I didn't know what to think about the discrepancy other than maybe their parents influenced them, and they thought they were saying the right thing.

So we got to work on the poster. We drew graphs to show the results of the surveys. The charts looked good, but didn't tell much. We explained how we averaged the choices for the four days. In the information part, we mentioned the salad numbers. More importantly, we mentioned the amount of soda chosen and the fact that it shouldn't have been an option. We also reported the number of students who didn't take the required number of choices.

It was OK, but nothing as interesting as our new addition to the poster. Here we used schoollunchbox.org as our source. We made lists of healthy lunches that were listed on the site. We explained the guidelines school cafeterias were supposed to follow. Then we showed the menus from our school. We didn't use any names, but in the summary we concluded our cafeteria lunches needed to be more like the ones on schoollunchbox.org.

I knew this information would drive Mrs. Nunley and Mrs. Reardon crazy, and I worried about what they might say to Mr. Kohla. But we had told him about schoollunchbox.org, and he never said a word against it.

Mom got home just as we were finishing.

"Mom, this is Becky Albright."

"It's nice to meet you Becky; RJ talks about you all the time." I turned bright red.

"Nice to meet you Mrs. Johnson," said Becky. "It's been fun getting to know RJ while we worked on this project."

"Yes," said Mom, "tell me about the project."

So we did. We told her what information we had found, where we found it, and the conclusions we made. We did not tell her *all* of the details.

"Well, I'm really impressed," Mom said. "I know I learned a lot, although I've heard most of this before. But I will admit that I don't follow these guidelines as much as I should. I will have to work harder on making our meals better."

"I hope you will come to the science fair tomorrow night," Becky said.

"I wouldn't miss it. I took the night off from work."

I hoped Mom would not regret that decision.

CHAPTER FIFTY-NINE

"Welcome back. This is Celia Roberts with the news. Tonight we have more to report on the quickly developing story on school lunches. Yesterday a lengthy document, reportedly from the SchoolMeals division of the food giant AgraInc, was published in papers across the country. The report explains the process food goes through before it reaches school cafeterias in our nation. Still following that story is our reporter, Sean Bernard, who is on site. Sean?"

"Thanks, Celia. Most of us have read the articles in the newspapers. If the documents are accurate, there seems to be a serious disconnect between what we want and believe school cafeterias are serving and reality. I am standing in front of the AgraInc building. They are the major provider of food products for our school lunch programs. I asked to meet with the president of AgraInc to discuss this and other information we have received in the last few days, but he refused the meeting. I then asked to meet with someone from SchoolMeals, which is the division of AgraInc directly involved with the school lunch programs. Again, I was refused. I asked if there was anyone who would speak to me, and I was again told no. They mentioned their attorneys would have a comment, but they could not tell me when.

"The documents were lengthy and technical. They seemed to focus on the act of "processing" food for the school lunch program. Like you, I have seen these documents, but I know that when I read the information, I had many questions, as I believe you do too. So I asked Dr. Susan Thibdeau, who is a biology professor at Columbia University and specializes in nutrition, to help us out. She graciously agreed and is here with us now.

"Dr. Thibdeau, much of this report is technical, but it is clear at least to me that it indicates some problems in the delivery of food to school lunch programs."

"You are absolutely correct, Sean. School lunch programs have not met the guidelines established by the government. Kids who eat school lunches have higher rates of obesity than kids who do not, and this is in part due to commodity processing."

"Would you explain that, Doctor."

"Of course. The US government provides school districts with more than 180 different food items every year, which is valued at over one billion dollars. These foods are much less expensive, so schools can save money by purchasing them. The problem with this situation is twofold. First, the majority of these items—I believe it's over 80 percent—are meat and cheese products, which are loaded with fat, particularly saturated fat, and sodium."

"Secondly, schools can purchase these food items through a commodity "processor," which transforms them into actual meal items. These are less expensive and favored by the kids, so more school lunches are sold. In the processing, fruits become fruit pies and grains become cookies and pastries, for just a few examples. These foods contain fewer nutrients and more saturated fats and sugars, which make them even worse choices for the kids."

"This sounds like it should be illegal, Doctor."

"It should be, but it is not. Unethical in my opinion, but legal. These processing companies, of which AgraInc is the largest, are not regulated. Consequently, they can add whatever they want without oversight."

"Let me be sure, Doctor, that I am hearing you correctly. Are you saying the government oversees the school lunch program and the commodity program but not the processing of the foods?"

"Sadly, Sean, your hearing is just fine. So we have the government programs designed to help make and keep our kids healthy, but as you have reported less than 8 percent of schools met the dietary guidelines."

"So who do you blame, Doctor? The agencies who are not doing a decent job of oversight or the food companies who make millions feeding our kids junk?"

"I'm a scientist, Sean, not a politician. I am simply appalled these practices have gone on for years. Scientists have been telling people about it, but nothing has changed. Maybe now something will."

"I certainly hope so, Doctor. Thanks for sharing your expertise."

"You're welcome."

"By the way, I should add that although we have heard next to nothing from AgraInc, there have been threats of lawsuits against the papers that published these documents and those who provided the documents to the papers. I should also add that at no time has anyone denied the validity of these documents. The newspapers have refused to reveal where the information originated from, but they assure us they have checked the sources and believe them to be genuine."

"Back to you, Celia."

CHAPTER SIXTY

FRIDAY, MAY 20
RJ AND BECKY

Friday after school, I went over to Becky's house. We wanted to look at the posters one last time and check that we had everything we needed before the science fair that night.

"I think I should take along some pages from schoollunchbox. org, along with the names of the doctors who contribute to the site," said Becky.

"Good idea. Some of the parents there might want to know who the people are who we quote," I agreed.

"What do you think Mrs. Reardon will do when she sees this part about the cafeteria menus?" she asked.

"I don't think she'll do much in front of all the parents. If anything, we'll probably get yelled at later," I answered.

"Well, it doesn't matter to me. I know our parents will be behind us."

"I hope they don't have to be."

Becky looked thoughtful for a moment. "Me neither," she said. "But on the other hand, with all the stories in the newspapers about school lunches and kids' health, I don't know."

"Isn't it interesting," she continued, "we wound up doing a project about something that turns out to be the biggest news story of the year?" She looked at me with an inquisitive expression.

"I know," I said, "what a coincidence."

"You think?" she asked. "Doesn't your brother go to Columbia University where the head of 8th Day works? Do you think he knows him?"

"Dunno," I said honestly. "It's a big school."

"Wouldn't it be cool if your brother was like an undercover agent for 8th Day?" she said.

"I don't think my mom would think so."

Becky had another funny look on her face. "Maybe we could be members of 8th Day. That would be way cool. Of course, no one could know."

"They'd never use kids as young as us," I lied. "Besides, what could we do?"

"Well, the things we got from the witch's office might have helped them. I mean, how strange is that? We find those memos and the same kind of memos show up all over the country. Don't you think that's weird?"

"Very," I said. *Not so strange*, I thought to myself. "I'm going home to get something to eat," I said to change the subject. "I'll be back about fifteen minutes before we're supposed to be there."

"Good," she answered. "But don't hurry. I want us to be late enough so the place is full of parents. That way if Mrs. Reardon tries anything, the parents will be watching."

I went home and ate dinner. Mom wasn't home yet, but she left me some roasted chicken, mashed potatoes, and spinach to warm up in the microwave. I had forgotten how much I liked spinach. Mom decided that if I were doing a project on healthy eating, she wanted to be part of it. I went to grab a soda and stopped. Instead I drank a glass of milk.

I put on my only coat and tie and went to Becky's house.

"My Dad says our project looks great," she told me. "He had to go over to the university to check on a late lab, but he told me he would come right over to the school afterward."

We got our things together and walked down to the school five minutes before the science fair opened.

The parking lot was almost full, and cars were still arriving. We went in the entryway. There was a desk by the door. Mrs. Cooney, the PTA president, was sitting behind the desk. She had the locations for all the exhibits. She was a chubby woman with dark hair and was always smiling.

"Oh, Becky and RJ. We were wondering where you were," she said.

"I slowed us up a bit," said Becky.

"No problem. The eighth grade is in the library. You have station thirteen. I hope that's good luck," she laughed.

I doubted it, but didn't say anything.

We took all of our project materials into the library and found our table. I was glad to see Mrs. Reardon wasn't there. She probably started with the sixth graders. Mr. Kohla was on the other side of the room talking to some parents.

We went right to work and set up our posters.

Congress enacted a law in 1995 requiring school meals to comply with the recommendations of the Dietary Guidelines for Americans. This law established standards that are consistent with the Dietary Guidelines for Americans.

What are the Dietary Guidelines for Americans?

❖Eat a variety of foods

❖Balance the food you eat with physical activity

❖Choose a diet with plenty of grain products, vegetables and fruits

❖Choose a diet low in fat, saturated fat, and cholesterol

❖Choose a diet moderate in sugars

❖Choose a diet moderate in salt and sodium

Every school lunch must provide the following foods in the indicated amounts.

5 Food Categories	Portion Size
8 ounces Milk	8 ounces skim or 1%
1 Fruit / Vegetable	¾ cup
2 Fruit / Vegetable	¾ cup
Protein	2 ounces meat/fish 1 egg or 2 Tablespoons P B
Grain	1 per day

SCHOOL LUNCH CHOICES SURVEY
Becky Albright, RJ Johnson
Eight Grade Science Fair Blalock Middle School
36 Students were asked the following questions

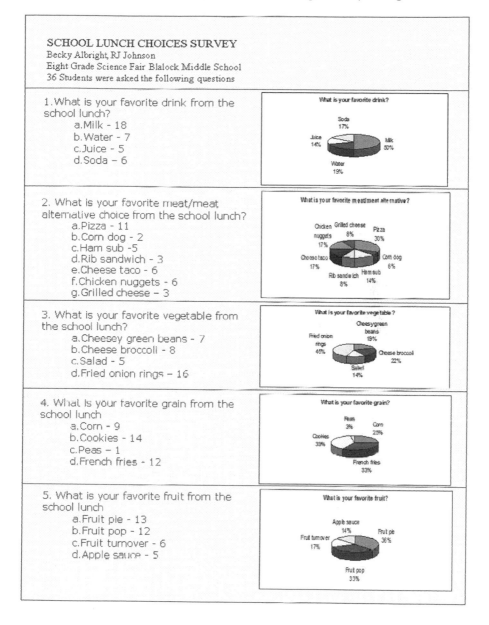

1. What is your favorite drink from the school lunch?
    a. Milk - 18
    b. Water - 7
    c. Juice - 5
    d. Soda – 6

2. What is your favorite meat/meat alternative choice from the school lunch?
    a. Pizza - 11
    b. Corn dog - 2
    c. Ham sub -5
    d. Rib sandwich - 3
    e. Cheese taco - 6
    f. Chicken nuggets - 6
    g. Grilled cheese – 3

3. What is your favorite vegetable from the school lunch?
    a. Cheesey green beans - 7
    b. Cheese broccoli - 8
    c. Salad - 5
    d. Fried onion rings – 16

4. What is your favorite grain from the school lunch
    a. Corn - 9
    b. Cookies - 14
    c. Peas – 1
    d. French fries - 12

5. What is your favorite fruit from the school lunch
    a. Fruit pie - 13
    b. Fruit pop - 12
    c. Fruit turnover - 6
    d. Apple sauce - 5

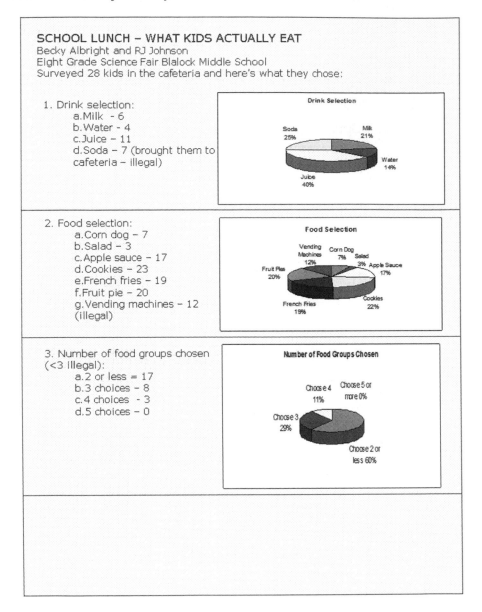

SCHOOL LUNCH – WHAT KIDS ACTUALLY EAT
Becky Albright and RJ Johnson
Eight Grade Science Fair Blalock Middle School
Surveyed 28 kids in the cafeteria and here's what they chose:

1. Drink selection:
    a. Milk - 6
    b. Water - 4
    c. Juice – 11
    d. Soda – 7 (brought them to cafeteria – illegal)

2. Food selection:
    a. Corn dog – 7
    b. Salad – 3
    c. Apple sauce – 17
    d. Cookies – 23
    e. French fries – 19
    f. Fruit pie – 20
    g. Vending machines – 12 (illegal)

3. Number of food groups chosen (<3 illegal):
    a. 2 or less = 17
    b. 3 choices – 8
    c. 4 choices - 3
    d. 5 choices – 0

Within minutes, parents came by and started looking at and reading our presentation. They started asking us questions about how we got our information and what we thought about the lunches. Becky did most of the talking, but I pitched in when a crowd started to form around our table.

"I have been reading about lunches in the papers," one parent said to another.

"Me too," said another. "I guess I never thought it might be a problem here."

"We should ask the school board about this."

By this time, there were so many people around the table that I couldn't see past them. There was a little opening in the crowd and I heard a voice. "Coming through, please. Sorry, need to get by." I recognized the voice. It was Mrs. Reardon.

Here it comes, I thought.

She said excuse me to the parents and came up front. She looked at the report and read everything.

Becky and I stood still. Becky was smiling. I wasn't.

It was almost funny watching Mrs. Reardon. As she looked at and read the materials, she was getting angrier. It was like watching a thermometer getting redder and redder the further she read.

Finally she looked at the two of us. I was glad parents surrounded us.

"I knew you two were up to something. This is not what your report was supposed to be about."

"Oh, yes it is," said Becky politely. "It's about school lunches."

"Don't talk back to me," Mrs. Reardon said. There were some gasps from the parents.

"I didn't approve this part about the quality of our lunches."

"It was just something that came up in our research," I added.

"Don't you talk either, RJ. I would expect this from her but not you," she hissed.

"Don't talk to my daughter that way," I heard Dr. Albright's voice as he moved forward through the crowd.

"Or my son," Mom said. I hadn't seen her, but she was in the back somewhere.

Mrs. Reardon ignored them and looked at us. "Take this trash down right now."

"Don't touch it," Dr. Albright responded. He stood up front now. "If you want a fight, I'll give you one. If you remove that project, I'll have a lawyer at your door on Monday and the Board of Ed will hear about this tonight."

There was applause from some of the parents.

"I thought this was supposed to be about learning," one of the parents said. "Well, it looks like these kids have learned a lot."

I heard "you're right" and "yes" from the crowd.

Mrs. Reardon looked up. It was as if she had just realized where she was. She stood up tall, straightened her skirt, and pushed her way through the throng of parents. There was more applause.

Dr. Albright came over. Mom was at his side.

"Don't worry guys," he said. "She won't say anything to you. Too many witnesses." He smiled and pointed with his thumb to the rest of the crowd.

Then he leaned over and whispered to me, "You're quite the guy, RJ."

Mom gave me a hug and said she loved the project.

It was a busy evening. I was worried about Mr. Kohla. He came by later and didn't say a word; he just winked at us and smiled.

We didn't win any of the prizes.

CHAPTER SIXTY-ONE

MONDAY, MAY 23
GRACIELA

I had been working with Miss Fuentes for three weeks and enjoying it. I particularly liked chatting with kids from all over the country. I was surprised by how many of them had physical problems caused by or made worse by being overweight. There were quite a few who already had type 2 diabetes. They were on very strict diets and had to take insulin every day. And some kids had asthma; extra weight hurt them too. Sometimes when they tried to run or play, they had asthma attacks, and some wound up in the hospital. I listened and wrote back encouragement.

Miss Fuentes posted a new article every day educating kids on how to get and stay healthy. Whenever someone asked me a question I didn't understand, I talked to Miss Fuentes. Often she would give me articles or websites to share, but sometimes she advised me to tell them to see a doctor.

On this Monday evening, Miss Fuentes returned to her office after taking a phone call. She looked a little concerned.

"Is everything all right?" I asked.

She smiled as she always does.

"No, not really. It is just time for me to ask you to do something important again, and I always worry when I have to do this."

"What is it?" I asked.

"Let me remind you again: if you don't want to do this, I will not be disappointed."

"I understand," I said. "Please, tell me."

"I know you have been paying attention to the news about school lunches. And we have talked about it a lot."

"Yes, it seems in some ways very complicated, but it also seems pretty simple. People working for the school lunch programs across the country have not been doing a very good job. In fact, some people say they are criminals and should be arrested. I don't know about that."

"You are right," she said. "It is complicated, but also very important. It is one of the most important reasons 8th Day exists. Some important people in Washington and other places are arguing about this, and it is not certain they will change the lunches and make things better for the kids."

"Why wouldn't they?" I asked.

"Because some companies are making billions of dollars from the current situation, and they are not happy or very willing to change anything that might make them less money."

"But isn't the health of the kids most important?" I asked.

"Absolutely! But sometimes the adults need to be reminded. That's where you come in."

"Me?"

"Yes, the adults need to understand that kids care about this issue and want something done. So I would like you to write a letter to our BFFKids friends and ask them to do something."

"What?" I asked.

"Let me tell you."

CHAPTER SIXTY-TWO

WEDNESDAY, MAY 25
GRACIELA

Dear BFFKids Reader,

I have chosen to invite you to be part of something important for several reasons. First, you have been a loyal reader ever since the site opened. Secondly, you have shown a great interest in learning how to be healthy. Finally, you sound like a leader. Now I need your help. Kids everywhere need your help.

This Friday, May 27, I am asking you to be part of something to improve the health of kids everywhere. I am sure you have heard it on the news; there is a great concern that school lunches are not as good as they should be. In fact, in many cases, they can harm students who eat them. Right now, only adults are talking about this issue. I believe they need to hear from us—the ones who eat school lunches.

Here is what I need you to do. Ask the members of your class and other classes to join in an activity that will let adults know we care about our health. First, tell the students to keep the plan secret, even if they do not wish to take part. Use your computers or cell phones. Second, ask each student to come to school on Friday without lunches from home. Third, ask each student to make a sign. Ask them to print the word NO in bold, capital letters on a piece of standard, white computer paper. The word should be as big as possible. Next, when students go to lunch, they should have their signs in their pockets. They should line up as if to buy lunch and when the lunch line opens, they should turn toward the center of the cafeteria and open the signs. They should say nothing. Finally, when adults ask them what's going on, tell them the truth. Tell them you will not eat lunches because you know they are not good for you. Tell them you heard about this on the Internet. Also tell them you know what's been going on from the news, and you want them to know you are concerned. Do not identify yourself as the leader.

You may be the only one in your school who I am contacting, but there might be others as well. If you do not wish to participate, please say nothing of this.

Yours in good health,

BFFKids

Miss Fuentes finished reading the letter. She smiled and I knew she liked it.

"This is wonderful, Gracie," she said.

"Well, it was your idea," I replied.

"But you put it in your own words, and that will make this plan work much better."

"When do we send it out?" I asked.

"I will take care of that tonight," she said.

"But this has to happen on Friday. Isn't this a little late?"

"No, it's better not to have too much time between the letter and the action; we don't want people who might try to stop it to have time to thwart the plan."

"Then do it," I said.

CHAPTER SIXTY-THREE

MONDAY, MAY 23
KARSTAN

I don't watch a lot of news on TV. Basically, I could care less. But Uncle Jerry e-mailed me last week and told me to watch the story on TV, or read in the newspapers, about the school lunch business and the companies involved. Although I wasn't sure, I guessed Uncle Jerry was giving me a heads up about what I had given to the 8th Day people.

I enjoyed it. I thought it was hilarious that a bunch of kids had something to do with giving a big company a hard time. And I was happy that maybe some good would come from it. I am cynical sometimes. All I need to do is listen to my mom talk about some of the jerks her law firm works with. I've even heard her tell Dad that if it were up to her, she would dump a few of the clients. But she calls them cash cows, and it's hard to stop doing business with people who know how to make money.

I got home right after school and no one was there. Carmella had to take care of her daughter, so I had a few hours of my own. I thought I would settle in to *The Galaxy of Death* when I decided I had liked playing spy. So I went up to mom's room and turned on her computer. I went back into her documents and found AgraInc again. They seemed to be the bad guys right now.

But what I really wanted to know was what was in that School-Meals folder and if it had anything to do with what was going on in the papers. So I went to the folder and opened it this time. There were mucho documents. I looked around some and most of the information didn't make sense to me. But then I saw one titled processing, and I remembered that was something mentioned on TV. I looked at it, but it was way too technical for me. However, it made me feel like I was part of something important. It looks like this was what all the noise was about.

But I wasn't going to waste my time reading it. I started to close out. When I got to the home page, I saw a mail icon blinking. It's a program Mom has to let her know immediately when an e-mail comes in. I couldn't resist. I opened it. It was from some guy named Jeffrey Tobin, and he was like an assistant to the director of SchoolMeals. The e-mail was actually sent to bunches of people. What Mom was getting was a copy. I opened the e-mail. I couldn't believe what I read. I sat still for a moment when I finished. Then I went to my computer, immediately opened Facebook, and looked for Lamar. I hoped he was there. I waited an hour, but he finally got on. I told him he needed to see something and I sent the e-mail along.

Then I went to my room and sat quietly. I was trying to think of a reason my mom would work for those people.

CHAPTER SIXTY-FOUR

Dear Visitors,

Welcome to 8th Day. Please feel free to look at any or all of our pages. We hope you will find the information helpful. In recent weeks AgraInc has accused us of illegally obtaining and leaking documents and memos about the operations of companies in the food industry and particularly AgraInc. More specifically the leaked information points to a questionable relationship between the companies and the managers of school lunch programs in the country. They have threatened to bring suit against us. Our attorneys have advised us not to comment, and we will not.

However, we have had an internal communication at AgraInc, specifically the SchoolMeals division, come into our possession. It was given to us anonymously. We have checked with sources within AgraInc who have verified this communication. They have asked not to be identified, and we have agreed. The content of this communication is so startling we feel it necessary to bring it into the light. For that reason we are posting it here. We expect AgraInc to object and attempt to stop us, but we are confident if this goes to the judicial system, we will prevail.

Below, please find the communication.

To: SchoolMeals Division Members
From: Jeremy Tobin, Assistant to the Director
Re: Recent Attack

I know all of us have watched in dismay the attacks against our company and specifically this division. In order for us to weather this storm, we must remain a team. To that end, remember no member of this division should talk to any member of the media or private individuals concerning the reports about our operation and the accusations being made. To do so would mean immediate termination without benefits. I am sure I need not remind you that we have one and only one obligation, and that is to our shareholders. Our only reason for existing is to show a profit and, indeed, to do whatever necessary to be as profitable as possible. We are not the government. We are not the school systems. We owe neither any obligation. This is a free market economy, and we can and should do whatever is necessary to succeed for our shareholders.

While we may care about the health of the young people in this country, they are not our responsibility. Have they no parents? Have they no teachers? Are the adults in their lives too stupid or lazy to educate their charges in healthy eating? If their choices cause them harm, then it has been their choice. It has been clear to all of us in the industry that for at least the last twenty years, parents have not been at home for, nor do they monitor what their children do, let alone what they eat.

At this time, we must close ranks.

CHAPTER SIXTY-FIVE

SUNDAY, MAY 29
NBC NEWS, NEW YORK

"Good evening. This is Celia Roberts from New York. Well, just when you thought it couldn't get worse, it has. Yesterday, the group 8th Day, which has been implicated in the release of documents criticizing several food companies and their relationship with the school lunch programs, posted a memo on it's website allegedly from Jeremy Tobin, the assistant director of SchoolMeals, a division of AgraInc. It is explosive. If you haven't read it yet, you need to. The memo states that SchoolMeals and the mother company AgraInc bear no responsibility for what children eat in school even though they are the providers of that food. The writer goes on to suggest that the parents and teachers are too stupid or lazy to teach their kids what to eat. This, needless to say, has not set well with the public. Since the posting, there have been rallies and protests at the AgraInc building. Several people have been arrested for trespassing and attempting to enter the building. The police set up barricades to get the few employees of AgraInc who were working this weekend out of the building. One of the protesters carried a sign emblazoned with the slogan: Not More Money—More of a Future.

"You will remember last Friday middle school students across the nation boycotted the school lunches. If they are so concerned about healthy food, perhaps the adults had better pay attention.

"There will certainly be more on this story during the week. Tune in to hear Sean Bernard, who has covered this story from the beginning."

CHAPTER SIXTY-SIX

TUESDAY, MAY 31
NBC NEWS, NEW YORK

"Good evening, this is Sean Bernard from New York. It's been a busy two days. Since the posting of the SchoolMeals e-mail, AgraInc, the huge food conglomerate, has filed suit against 8th Day and its head Dr. Oteri, a professor at Columbia University, claiming malicious libel. The amount of the suit is not yet known. In addition, AgraInc wants criminal charges brought against Dr. Oteri and 8th Day for theft and trespassing. Dr. Oteri, speaking for the organization, has denied all charges. AgraInc has tried to paint Dr. Oteri as an unstable radical whose scientific theories should be questioned. In reaction, professors of biology from every state have made public statements supporting Dr. Oteri. The heads of the biology departments at Stanford, UCLA, Yale, Johns Hopkins, and other universities have written letters to the attorney general of New York and the president of the United States in support of Dr. Oteri.

"As this goes on, the protests at the AgraInc building have grown larger and more aggressive. In the last two days, more than thirty people have been arrested. The mayor is calling upon the people of New York to calm down and let the courts decide what needs to happen.

"Finally, the president stepped in. He has called for a Congressional Committee to be appointed. The committee will have the power to subpoena. Senator McDonald of Massachusetts will chair the committee. Just an hour ago, the senator told the press that he will subpoena members of 8th Day, employees of AgraInc, and any other organizations involved in the delivery of food to the school lunch program. He promises to find out the truth when these individuals testify under oath to the Congressional Committee. When asked what would happen if anyone chose not to testify or used the fifth amendment shield, he said, 'They will then be in contempt of the US Congress, and believe me, that had better not happen.'"

CHAPTER SIXTY-SEVEN

WASHINGTON, DC

All of us were watching the press conference on television. There were two old men and an old woman sitting at a long table with microphones and nameplates in front of them. The one on the left was Attorney General Jonathan Witaker. The one on the right was Surgeon General Dr. Anne Brooks. In the middle sat Vice President Andrew Corr.

The vice president began. "Welcome. The president asked us to address the nation concerning the recent incidents, of which I am sure you are all aware, and the positions this administration and legislative bodies will be taking.

"First, let me introduce Dr. Brooks, the surgeon general of the United States."

"Thank you, Mr. Vice President. Over the course of the last several months, we have all read about the events that occurred in our public schools. These events have ranged from the distribution of materials concerning the health of the nation's children, to sit-in's where students refused to eat lunches provided by their schools. In addition to this, there have been similar actions taken at universities and colleges across the country. Many people blame these actions, and in some cases disruptions, on the organization known as 8th Day.

"Let me start by saying that although at times some of the methods allegedly used by 8th Day may have been marginally legal, the office of The Surgeon General stands arm-in-arm with 8th Day in the common goal to protect our children from disease and distress caused by food consumed from suppliers who knew the provided products were counter to what we know as healthy for young bodies.

"To that end, this office has reviewed existing regulations for school lunch programs, and we have directed the agencies involved to coordinate their efforts and guarantee the effective oversight of these programs to ensure healthier lunches for our children. Both houses of the US Congress are prepared to pass further legislation, particularly in the area of commodity processing, to ensure a higher standard for our children's school lunches.

"Finally, as we know, documents have become public clearly indicating that many parts of our food industries have consciously been aware that their products were not in the best interest of their customers: our children. To those companies and individuals, I say, shame on you. What you have done is disgraceful.

"However, they alone were not the problem. Clearly we as parents share the blame as well. And let me be clear, no amount of legislation can change the terrible situation in which we find ourselves unless parents take an increasingly aggressive role in seeing to it that our children's health comes first."

"Thank you, Mr. Vice President."

"Thank you, Dr. Brooks. Now we will hear from Jonathan Witaker, attorney general of the United States."

"Thank you, Mr. Vice President. In the last months, this office has continually tracked the events that have brought us to this point. 8th Day has never denied its mission to change how we as a nation feed our children. The actions toward this goal have to this point been within the law. Although some protestors have been arrested for failure to disperse, nothing more serious has been proven. The accusations that 8th Day has made false and slanderous claims simply have no basis. Information and documents leaked to the press clearly show the claims made by 8th Day have been accurate. The defamation law suits brought against individuals and the organization 8th Day have been dropped. It is still unclear as to how these documents got into public hands, but it is also irrelevant. Members of the food industry have given testimony that the information in the documents was factual. Needless to say, many members of the industry have resigned or been released. This office will continue its investigation and promises legal action wherever appropriate."

There was cheering in the room. The vice president asked for quiet.

"I wish to thank all of those people who worked long and hard on this important issue.

"We see no reason to waste taxpayer's money continuing to look for those individuals who leaked the information prompting our investigation. Many believe they are heroes."

FINAL CHAPTER

RJ felt relieved; the mission was complete and everyone was safe. I was most worried about Lamar because he did so much with the computer stuff. I went to my computer and signed on our communications site. I was certain they'd all be there. Within five minutes Lamar, Gracie, and K-Man were online, all wearing big smiles.

"Congratulations, team," Lamar said. "We're heroes!" Everyone laughed.

"Don't feel like a hero," Karstan replied. "But it's good news that my mom wasn't working on all those companies, and she told me she's happy her firm is dropping them as a client. You know, I'm glad my little part helped. I never understood what Uncle Jerry was talking about when he said everyone has a responsibility to know about and pay attention to what the government and businesses do."

"I'm just glad it's over," said Gracie. "I've got to get back to my real schoolwork. And I'm happy to be part of a country where all the people have a chance to make a difference. I am amazed that our boycott was so effective, even though it was just kids."

"I was surprised," Lamar said, "to find there were such important issues right in front of me. And I'm thrilled my abilities were important in this whole adventure. We all made an incredible difference. I now know that my computer skills go beyond playing games."

"Yeah," I said, "it's gonna be a lot less exciting around here now. But I have learned so many important things, like how to take care of my health and how to stand up for what I think is right even when I'm scared.

"Here's to the Gang of Four: always friends and friends to everyone."

We signed off, and I wondered if I would ever see them again.

Dr. Jane Pentz is CEO of Lifestyle Management Associates and founder of the non-profit organization, The American Academy of Sports Dietitians and Nutritionists. Pentz is the author of a nutrition textbook and several nutrition books as part of continuing education programs for professionals, and has also published a children's nutrition curriculum that features children's books aimed at introducing nutritional concepts. She holds a Ph.D. in nutritional biochemistry from Tufts University. Doug Dwyer is a career educator who has been a teacher and school administrator from kindergarten to graduate school, working in the Northeast and the South. For ten years, he wrote and delivered commentary for NPR stations with audiences in New York, Connecticut and Tennessee. He has also taught writing to college students. No: Book One of the 8th Day Series is their first collaborative work. Visit the authors at www.bffkids.org.

Made in the USA
Charleston, SC
21 March 2012